NO END IN SIGHT

ON BEHALF OF DEATH
BOOK TEN

E.G. STONE

TARNEY BRAE CREATIVE ENDEAVOURS

For my Family

CONTENTS

PREFACE

To those fans of Arthurian legend who are excited about my exploration of the Fisher King, I warn you now that this is absolutely and entirely inaccurate. I started out by trying to remain close to the legend and then decided that the legend needed to fit my book. From here on in, expect no accuracy in that regard. Actually, this is fantasy, and from my mind, no less, so I wouldn't expect much accuracy to any sort of legend or myth at all. Sorry.

- E.G. Stone

CHAPTER 1

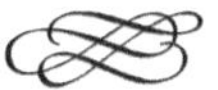

I was late. Not just five minutes late, but over an hour late. Normally, I wouldn't worry too much about it; marketing was rarely a job that involved punctual daily schedules. But when it was my monthly dinner with my mother—who terrified both Life and Death—then being late was akin to a death sentence.

Perhaps literally.

"This is your fault," I growled at Baz as we hurried down the street.

"Come on, Cal, how could *I* know that the portal wasn't calibrated properly?" my cousin complained.

"Because you're the one responsible for calibrating it!" I wiped at my face, feeling a drop of moisture that hadn't been there moments before. A quick glance upward had another raindrop splatting right on the lens of my glasses. Great. Just great.

Some days, I hated London. When I was running late, there were inevitably no cabs to be found, not even a rideshare available, *and* the tube was under maintenance, not to mention that now it was raining. I really, really hated London.

I skidded around the corner to my mother's street and immediately slowed my pace. I straightened my tie, tugged at my vest, adjusted my jacket, and took a few calming breaths. Baz, on the other hand, just squinted up at the sky. "Do you know, that storm doesn't look normal."

I ignored him and walked up to my mother's front door with as much dignity as possible, given that the rain was starting to fall in earnest. I knocked. The door swung open.

"Calvin Montgomery Thorpe, you are late." My mother, tall, her brown hair swept up in a neat chignon, wearing wide-legged trousers and a loose silk blouse in true sartorial elegance, was intimidating at the best of times. When I was late? She was positively terrifying.

"Hello, Mother." I leaned in, kissing her cheek. "I brought Baz."

My cousin, the immortal embodiment of Justice, fairly cowered before my mother. "Hi, Aunt Teresa.

We would have brought some wine, but, ah, there was a mishap with the portal, and—"

"Get down!" my mother screamed. She grabbed my arm, grabbed Baz by the collar of his shirt, and dragged us both through the door. The lightning bolt that had been aiming for one or both of us cracked ineffectively against the pavement. I could feel the magic tingling through my teeth, but it couldn't cross the barrier of the threshold.

The sky let out a furious rumble, something like a hiss and a snarl. The clouds flashed a shade of orange that was definitely not seen in any natural storm. Lightning streaked across the sky, illuminating the shape of a massive creature. Then, with a sound that fairly rattled the world, everything went back to how it should be.

Rain splattered on the scorched pavement, getting the entryway wet.

"W-was that a *dragon?*" Baz nearly screeched. His reddish hair was sticking up at all angles and he looked like he'd nearly had a heart attack.

I surreptitiously smoothed down my own hair, just in case. "Calm, please, Baz. You know full well that abject panic will do no one any good in a situation such as—"

"Oh, stuff it. Just because you're no longer possessed of human panic doesn't mean that I can't indulge."

"Boys," my mother said. She was unusually pale, and I detected a faint tremor in her hand, which was still clutching my sleeve. It was the most distressed I'd ever seen my mother. In fact…

"You *screamed*," I said, frowning. "You've never even so much as raised your voice at me."

My mother blinked. She released my sleeve, took in the rain now spilling into her house, and promptly slammed the door. "I think we should talk," she said, turning away from us. "Clean your-selves up and we'll have dinner. Shoes off, please. I don't need dirty water spreading all over the house."

She vanished into the kitchen.

Baz and I gaped at each other. We both looked towards the kitchen, then back.

"Maybe she's just had a bad day?" I suggested.

"Seriously? That was a *dragon*. I think that might transcend having a bad day."

"So…do you want to tell her about my losing my humanity and being Death's heir, or shall I?"

Baz punched me in the arm. "Take off your shoes and don't be an idiot."

I left my shoes on the mat and followed my cousin into the kitchen. It would be up to me to break my news to my mother, then, and I had a feeling it wasn't going to go well. Not after whatever had just happened. Whatever that was.

DINNER WAS a monthly affair that had begun shortly after my mother learned that I hadn't actually been killed, but hired on by Death to be his marketing agent. Since then, things had gotten more complicated. I became a Grim Reaper, a sort of magical entity that stood between Life and Death. I had accidentally gotten my cousin a job as Justice. There were various other, ah, incidents as well, the latest leaving me without whatever remained of my humanity and therefore in line to be the next Death.

Through all of this, monthly dinners with my mother had been constant.

They always started with my mother taking a good look at me and then declaring me either acceptably dressed—a true compliment—or looking terrible—the more common pronouncement. Then, we would dish up whatever food had been ordered from the local Indian restaurant, as neither my mother nor I could cook and indulge in banal discussions of her job at the local library or my marketing work.

Baz attended on most occasions, which invariably made the dinners far more entertaining. My cousin had lived in my family house since we were teenagers and his own parents kicked him out for getting expelled. Twice. He and "Aunt Teresa" were more adversarial than otherwise, but it was a cheerful thing born of Baz's incomprehensible chaos and my mother's, well, dislike of incomprehensible chaos.

Tonight, though, we dispensed entirely with the personal appraisals. We dished out the food in complete silence, and when we'd all had enough of silently poking at our plates, all broke out talking at once.

Baz, of course, was the loudest. "That was a freaking *dragon!*"

"Cal, kindly explain what your cousin meant by you not being possessed of human panic." My mother managed to cut through Baz's declaration with pure steel.

"What do you know about the Fisher King?" I asked. Both my mother and Baz turned to me, looking confused.

"The Arthurian legend?" Baz asked.

My mother rolled her eyes. "It's far more than a mere 'Arthurian' legend. It has origins that date back to the early days of Wales and Scotland, with the grail sometimes being considered a cauldron, and the guardian losing his head. The Percival and Galahad versions of the story come much later."

"Uh...what? What does a grail have to do with

the Fisher King?" I asked around a mouthful of curry. I received a withering look from my mother for that. I swallowed my food, the spice hitting me all at once. Eyes watering, I repeated my question.

She took a delicate sip of her wine, studying me. "Very well. I will answer your questions first and then you shall answer mine."

Baz and I nodded eagerly.

"The Fisher King is a legend that dates back more than a thousand years. Now it is most commonly associated with Arthurian lore and the search for the holy grail. However, it first began as a more…wild tale. Legend says that the Fisher King is possessed of a cauldron—or a grail—that can heal and sometimes resurrect the dead. The cup of life. However, he is wounded in the thigh—a euphemism for being infertile in medieval times—"

"I didn't need to know that," Baz muttered, earning a severe glance.

"He is unable to produce an heir and therefore his line and sacred guardianship of this cauldron will end. His lands are tied to his health, and so they suffer for it. The only salvation for the Fisher King is to have someone, usually a hero archetype, come and fulfil a quest or answer a question which will restore his health and his lands. Then he will bestow the cauldron, or grail, upon the hero. Sometimes. The legends are a bit unclear as to what happens once the lands are restored. Wealth, glory, success, power, it's all a bit…muddled in the various retellings. Later legends have him bringing down the curse on his lands not through infertility, but being struck by the Lance of Longinus, the spear which pierced Christ's side. Whatever telling you wish to follow, the end result is the same: a hero must fulfil some task for the Fisher King to restore his kingdom and gain control of the cauldron or grail."

I winced. I'd learned, from a Fae lord known as the Shadow King, that the other Reapers were not gone from this world, but trapped. The only way to rescue them was to venture past the land of dragons and seek the Fisher King. Which, according to my mother, meant a quest of some sort. I *hated* quests. They inevitably ended up with more chaos and the ruination of my wardrobe.

Death had also made the rescue of the Reapers my first task as his apprentice.

He had been quite insistent about it, too. Insistent was perhaps the wrong word. Bringing down the sky in a fit of fire and fury was more accurate. Whoever had trapped the Reapers had acted against both Life and Death. Needless to say, he was not pleased.

"Medieval history is complicated," Baz

complained, stuffing his mouth with samosas. He had never done well in history class.

"That's what happens when you get people retelling and reshaping myths to their own desires. I don't dare contemplate what this modern wave of 'fairytale retellings' will do to future historical records." My mother was an avid reader, and I had been on the receiving end of her rants regarding the decline of civilisation before. It didn't stop her from devouring the latest romance novels, though.

"Now, I believe I have been more than patient, Cal. Kindly explain what your cousin meant regarding your humanity."

I felt my heart beating loudly in my chest. I rubbed my sternum, trying to best figure out how to explain things to my mother. "So…ah…"

"Without prevaricating, if you please."

"A while back, Death lost my soul. As you know. Well, I went on a quest to get it back, and in doing so I had to take Death's heart along as a beacon to attract Fate, since she was the only person who knew where my soul was. There was an…incident, and I had to, ah, put Death's heart next to my own in order to protect it from an angry witch who was trying to kill my soul. Anyways, as you know, I got my soul back, but I couldn't remove Death's heart because it was now part of me and…uh…" I took a breath, studying the woodgrain of the table with great interest. "A couple of months ago, I got put under a blood spell by, er, my doppelgänger who was trying to steal my humanity so that he could have my life, which he would have had except for the interference of Fate, only it ended badly and I had to use my Reaper powers on him and killed him, only I was still connected to him by blood magic, so IendedupkillingoffmyhumanityandnowI'mheirtoDeath."

My mother took another sip of wine. She inhaled through her nose, as if sampling the bouquet of the cheap corner store liquor. Then, ever so carefully, she set the glass on the table. Adjusted it so that it was in perfect alignment with the dinner plate.

"I believe I taught you to enunciate, Calvin," she said carefully. "It helps to prevent miscommunication in situations such as this. For example, I believe I just heard you say that *you* destroyed your own humanity and are now the heir to Death."

"That's correct."

My mother quirked one perfectly sculpted brow. "I wasn't aware that Death required an heir."

"Everything dies," I murmured. "By taking Death's heart into me, I set off a chain of events that culminated with my loss of humanity. I am...I am now a force of the universe, and there is no space for me except as Death's heir. Therefore, one day, he will simply fade away and I will take his place. We don't know when. And Life has to find her replacement, because she's tied to this Death. And…and…I'm sorry I didn't tell you earlier."

"Quite right, you should be sorry," my mother snapped, once again showing more emotion than I'd ever seen her display. "We may not have a conventional familial situation, but I am still your mother. I would prefer to know these things."

"In any case, Death has set my first task as finding the Fisher King," I said. "I have to go beyond the land of dragons and—"

"Yes," Baz said, propping his elbows on the table and earning a sharp look from my mother. "Speaking of dragons, what was that all about at the door?"

My mother reached for her wine glass, but her hand was shaking and she knocked it over instead. I'd never seen her clumsy. Never.

She stared at the pool of red on the table like she'd spilled blood there. She didn't reach for a napkin or towel, just watched the wine pool onto the table. "I…may have, accidentally, angered the dragons. Severely."

"How?" Baz asked while I mopped up the spilled wine with a napkin. "I mean, last time we saw dragons, you saved a whole clutch of their eggs, which seems kind of significant. Especially since you're some sort of mythical Knight or something."

My mother winced. "Your great aunt Elspeth died."

I blanked. There were a great many relatives of the Thorpe clan, and frankly, I had a terrible time keeping track of them all. Family reunions were something I avoided with great relish.

Baz, on the other hand, just nodded. "Great Aunt Elspeth, with the bizarre collection of weapons?"

Okay, I *definitely* would have remembered her. "Did I know her?"

"She was my aunt on my mother's side. I think she visited once or twice. Certainly after you went away to university." My mother shook her head. "Always an eccentric. Collected weaponry from history, everything from slingshots that were nearly dissolved with age to rifles from the 1930s criminals that ran amok in the States at the time."

I shuddered, having had personal experience with the spirit of one of those criminals.

"I liked the wall of swords," Baz said with a wistful smile. "Very threatening."

"It turned out she was a Knight. Her, ah, eccentricities were all to do with being the last Knight. Or so she thought. When she died, *I* became the last Knight, and somehow the dragons knew this. They have been hunting me down ever since." My mother rolled her eyes almost theatrically, as if it were nothing more significant than an infestation of squirrels.

"Why?" Surely she wasn't doing the dragons any harm here in London, working at a library.

"Supposedly, whoever kills the last Knight will be immediately elevated to leadership over the other dragons," my mother said.

Ah. Things were about to get even more complicated, then.

CHAPTER 2

"Hold on. Just wait a second. Being a Knight is a family thing, right? Shouldn't Cal be part of that?" Baz asked.

"Calvin has…other traits, likely inherited from his father," my mother said, looking me over. "Certainly he didn't get any of the Reaper abilities from *my* side of the family. Not to mention that now he's *done away with his humanity,* he can't be a Knight."

Being talked about as if I weren't there. Always a good thing. "Mother, perhaps I should talk to Death and see about getting you some protection."

"Aunt Teresa can take care of herself," Baz insisted. "Though…it is dragons we're dealing with."

My mother sighed. "Do you honestly think that any protection you or Death can provide would be sufficient? Knights and dragons are natural enemies, and there is no one in Elsewhere who can stand against them. Or have you forgotten the effect of dragons on the world?"

She had a point. The last time I'd encountered a dragon, they had nearly shattered reality just by crossing between realms. Just listening to their voice was painful. I doubted I could even *find* someone willing to stand up against a dragon, let alone do it long term while staying with my mother.

"So what do you propose?" I asked drily. "Shall I just leave you here to your fate? Let you carry a sword every time you leave the sanctuary of this house? Watch as the entire neighbourhood crumbles under the wrath of the dragons? Or do you intend to stay inside and have groceries delivered rather than get in their way?"

"Don't be impertinent," my mother snapped. She folded her napkin primly. "I'll be coming with you on your quest, naturally. The only way to deal with this is to go to the source, and since you must pass through the lands of the dragons to find the Fisher King, then I will accompany you."

Had I been drinking something, I would have choked. As it was, I nearly fell off my chair. Baz was silent for a moment, staring at me from behind his ever-present sunglasses. If I could see his eyes, I'm sure they would have been enormous. He made a choked sound in the back of his throat, then quickly excused himself and darted down the hall to the bathroom. Before the door slammed closed behind him, I heard howls of laughter.

"I don't see what's so funny," my mother said, scowling in his direction. "It's the logical thing to do."

"Logical, yes," I replied absently. All I could think was that *my mother* was going to accompany me on a quest set by Death himself. I wasn't sure if I should be terrified or humiliated, and for once I was grateful that my humanity had been stripped away or surely I would have melted into the floor by now. Instead, I managed to take several deep breaths and was left feeling merely discomfited.

"That settles it, then. I'll pack a bag and we can be off in the morning." Without waiting around to hear my response, my mother picked up her plate and vanished into the kitchen to clean up. I stared at the remains of my dinner, unable to move.

Eventually, my cousin returned, a grin splitting his face. "So. This will be an adventure, won't it?"

"Don't tell me you're coming, too," I grumbled. My mother would be bad enough. Baz, though at least familiar with Elsewhere, would make the situation untenable.

"Relax, I won't be there to snicker at you at inopportune times. I have an assignment from Life. Something to do with the Americans and their leadership. It's all a bit of a mess, frankly." Despite the casual tone he used, I could tell that Baz was concerned. I knew that he wasn't normally handed out assignments from Life directly. Those that were usually involved an assassination of some sort. I knew it had happened only a couple of times since my cousin took on the role of Justice, but every time it had, he'd come to my office thoroughly drunk and shaking.

We never talked about it once he sobered up.

"How am I going to explain this to Death?" I asked. "You know what he's like when dealing with her."

"I've never seen someone acquiesce so quickly before," Baz agreed. "It was like he's scared of her or something."

"Or something. Do you know, this might actually be a nightmare of mine?" I hesitated. "Back when I could dream."

It was one of the more noticeable differences in my new, full-immortal life. Dreams were now beyond my grasp. Occasionally, I fell asleep to memories playing behind my eyes, but full dreams? Even nightmares? Not anymore.

For a brief instant, I wondered what my life would have been like had I never met Death, never taken this job.

"Maybe this will be a good thing," Baz said after a moment. He sank into the seat next to me. "After all, it could be useful to have someone who even Death is scared of accompanying you on your quest."

"It's not that she's not capable, because if anyone could do what she wants, it's her, but…Baz, she is all that I have left of my human life. You are nearly as immortal as I. Neja? Yolanda? Agravane? Everything I have now came after my hiring by Death. If my mother is gone, then I won't have anything to tether me to this place."

My humanity was gone, irrevocably, but I still thought of the mortal realms as a place to call home. My mother was here, after all, demanding that I attend a monthly dinner.

"Cal, you're heir apparent for Death. I think you have more ties to this place—to every place—than anyone else besides Life and her heir, whoever that turns out to be. And while I understand and share your fear for Aunt Teresa in Elsewhere, she is more capable than most humans."

"She is still human, though," I murmured. "Fragile. I hadn't realised how fragile humans were until my own hold on such things was gone."

I didn't wait for a response. I wasn't sure there was one Baz could give that would make me feel better. No, it was simply best that I accept things. I could argue with my mother, leave her behind while she slept, do a thousand things that would keep her out of harm's way, but the truth was that she was in danger just remaining here. Bringing her to find the Fisher King with me might be dangerous, but at least I would be there with her.

And if her human frailty proved to be her undoing?

Then it was nothing more than the way of things. Everything died. I knew that.

But I would pretend otherwise for as long as I could.

I took the rest of the dishes into the kitchen and helped my mother wash up. She and I didn't speak, instead falling into a pattern that was comfortable and familiar. She washed, I dried, putting everything away neatly and exactly in its place. It was something I had done as soon as I was tall enough to reach the cabinets as a child, and countless times since. It was as familiar to me as breathing, a pattern so ingrained that I could likely move about with my eyes closed and—

I dropped a plate.

The familiar feeling fled until I was standing there, watching things happen without any real interest in them. Putting the dishes away was just an action. One belonging to someone now gone. The dropped plate wasn't startling, but just another event that would splinter off into a thousand other events, a thousand other possible futures.

"Ah," I said, a bit distantly. "Interesting."

"Interesting?" my mother bit out. "That was from my favourite set! And you stand there like it's nothing."

I saw more emotion flicker across her features than I'd seen since the day my father walked out on us. This whole evening, in fact, had been full of emotion. For her, for me, yet she was the one who looked like she might cry while I just stood there.

"I'll clean it up," I said after a moment, and I think we both knew it wasn't so much an apology as an acknowledgement of all that I'd lost, that gulf which now lay between us.

My mother nodded and dried her hands before slipping from the room. I heard murmuring from the hallway and left Baz and my mother to their conversation. I cleaned up the plate, finished the dishes, and fell asleep on the couch.

I didn't dream.

MORNING FOUND my mother and I ducking through London as we headed back to the portal which would take us to Elsewhere. Death had given me the key to a door that led to central London when I first started my monthly dinners with my mother. I knew there were other doors around the world, as well as many different portals between Elsewhere and other places, but this was the easiest to access, if not the most comfortable.

My mother was dressed in what I could only call Adventure Gear. She wore khaki coloured trousers that were stuffed into tall leather boots. She had a belt with many hooks, some with pouches on them, others with knives or flasks, or even a tin of matches. Between that, her linen shirt and leather jacket, I wasn't sure whether she best belonged in an Indiana Jones movie or at the site of an archeology dig. She wore a leather bag over her shoulder stuffed with who knows what. Oh, and then there was the sword that she had strapped across her back. That one earned a few strange looks, but thankfully, there was some sort of convention in town requiring costumes and people mostly ignored her.

I unlocked the storage closet in the tube station and we slipped inside before one of the workers could realise that we weren't meant to be there. Then, we stepped between realms.

It felt like a car trip over rough, unpaved roads.

My teeth clattered together, my bones rattled, and I invariably developed a desperate need to use the bathroom. A few seconds later and we were through the portal, emerging from the trunk of a tree on the edge of Death's estate.

My mother sniffed. "Surely that could be made more comfortable."

These were her first words in an entirely new—magical—realm, and that was what she chose? No comments on the silvery trees, or the mist which hugged our ankles? No mention of the manor house in the distance, or marvelling at the fact that we'd crossed realms at all?

My mother was certainly a character.

"I have to go pack a few things. Come with me." I hadn't planned on heading out on this quest right away; in fact, I had been actively procrastinating a bit. But one did not argue with my mother when she got it into her head to do something. So I led her across the manicured lawn edged in pollinator plants shrouded in mist and only realised that I was about to introduce my mother to my entire office staff once I'd opened the door.

Tempest, my pet miniature griffin ghost, barrelled out the door, flapping her wings furiously as she tried to escape the reaching grasp of Agravane. She was a ghost and could become incorporeal at will, but somehow the aurai—air elemental—had figured out how to capture her when she didn't want to be captured. Such as when she was destroying the office. This, invariably, led to chaos.

Tempest flew right through my mother and landed on my shoulder, letting out a smug screech. Agravane windmilled to a halt. "Cal! I didn't see you there. That horrible ghost has been sneaking into the snack bin."

"Ghost?" My mother raised an eyebrow.

I had forgotten that people unconnected to Death couldn't see ghosts. I was saved from having to explain that by the fact that Agravane was now gaping at my mother.

"Calvin?" she said pointedly. "Would you care to introduce us?"

"Mother, this is Agravane, my junior marketing agent. Agravane, this is—"

"A pleasure, Lady Thorpe," Agravane said, sweeping into a low bow. I couldn't tell if he was being sarcastic. "Cal has told us so much about you."

Many things I hoped he'd never repeat. "If you'll excuse us, Agravane," I growled, "I have to go pack."

"Of course!" With one swift motion, Agravane had his arm threaded through my mother's. "The Lady Thorpe and I will go tour the offices. I'm sure Yolanda would *love* to meet her!"

My rock troll assistant would probably faint when met with the intimidating scowl my mother wore as a standard expression. I vowed to pack as quickly as possible to avoid further humiliation. I decided discretion was the better part of valour and fled to ruminate over which shoes to take on this particular adventure.

I felt like my past and my present were about to collide, and I wasn't sure what to do about it.

CHAPTER 3

When I returned to my office, a rucksack over my shoulders, Yolanda and Agravane were sitting on the couch, laughing their heads off at some story my mother was telling.

"…I had to completely restock the break room before anyone could notice that it had been filled entirely with coffee and packets of crisps."

Well, piffle. My mother was telling stories about me. Unflattering stories about me.

"In my defence, I had just discovered the wonders of coffee as a teenager attending school. Try dissuading someone from that particular enjoyment." The words were cold, even, and yet they caused my employees to start laughing again. Riotously. I sighed.

"Cal, why have you not invited your mother before?" Yolanda asked, wiping tears from her eyes.

Agravane fixed me with a fierce grin. "Yes, Cal, why *haven't* you invited your mother before? She is a delight."

"Perhaps because she unsettles Death and Life is afraid of her?" I said. My mother looked smug with this pronouncement. Both Agravane and Yolanda shifted away ever so slightly. "I hate to cut this tête-à-tête short, but we really do need to get going."

"Indeed. No doubt the dragons have noticed that I'm no longer in London." My mother stood, brushing her trousers off. "I'm sure they'll figure out a way to track me—or you, Calvin—and it would be such a shame to destroy Death's house."

With that devastating snippet of information, my mother left Yolanda and Agravane gaping after her as she strode to the door. I sighed again. "Keep an eye on things, okay? And if I get out of cell range, let Neja know where I've gone?"

"Sure thing, boss," Agravane said, still staring after my mother.

Yolanda just bobbed her head in a vague nod.

I shifted my pack and followed after the last Knight, who had been let loose on an unsuspecting Elsewhere. At least the sword no longer looked out of place.

"Where to?" Mother asked, several strides down

the road leading to the edges of Death's estate and the beginnings of the lands of Life.

"We'll catch a wyvern to the Northern Reaches. It's goblin territory. Mountainous. Not quite as steep as some of the rock troll domains, but enough."

"Like the Scottish Highlands?"

Not at all. "Sure, if you want to think of it like that." If you expected the Highlands to be crawling with demonic sheep and goblins that liked to raid unsuspecting travellers. I'd not been there often, but each time I had gone usually resulted in my glasses getting thoroughly smashed. The few non-goblin creatures that lived up there were fierce warriors and had a fondness for drinking games that turned into brawls. As I discovered.

Mother and I walked down the road and it transitioned from the mist-shrouded greenery of Death's estate to the vibrant, colourful hues that surrounded Life. As the world shifted around us, my mother watched, but didn't seem all that shocked, or even interested.

"Why *have* you never invited me to meet your friends?" Mother asked after a while. I staggered, nearly falling over my very nice leather boots and into a pile of mud.

"What?" I gathered myself. "You never seemed particularly interested. I didn't want to inconvenience you."

She shot me a look that was equal parts hurt, anger, and superior disdain. "You are my son. It would not be an inconvenience to meet your friends."

"Really?"

"Don't sound so shocked, Calvin. All your life, have I not shown an interest in your doings?" Mother sniffed and lifted her chin, walking a couple of steps ahead. I said nothing, because the answer was, generally, "No."

She had been a good parent, don't get me wrong. But affection? Interest in my interests? They were not her skill set. She had payed far more attention to Baz when we were growing up, and that was only because he kept getting into trouble that was not easily solved without her assistance. She'd offered help when I asked, certainly, and she was there for me, should I need her, but she never encouraged me to need her.

We had a relationship of logic and mild attachment, my mother and I. We loved fiercely, but not openly.

And that, I think, was part of the problem.

"The wyvern station is just down there," I said, pointing to where the two-legged, winged beasts lay in a neat line, immense saddles on their back for passengers. They resembled dragons in general shape, but were much smaller and only semi-sentient. They certainly couldn't shake the fabric of existence with their voices. I wasn't even sure they had voices.

"Interesting. It would seem that whenever the wyverns and dragons developed distinct lines of evolution that they managed to be domesticated by people, rather unlike the dragons, who were usually doing the domestication." My mother walked faster, reaching the large, scaled beasts and examining them with a keen eye. "They haven't got the same musculature as dragons. Similar, but you can see here that the chest and shoulders are far more streamlined, likely because they use their wings as both legs and flying appendages."

"Keep back!" a short, stocky man snarled, poking my mother with a stick. "None of my creatures are for sale, and if you get any ideas, I'll rip your arms off and feed them to my beasts as lunch."

"I beg your pardon!" Mother reared back, visibly offended. "Sir, I have no interest in buying your beasts, as you say, and to imply that I would do them harm is highly offensive. There is no need to resort to threats. My son and I are merely here to purchase a ride."

The man—a beardless dwarf of halfling, most likely—curled his lip at my mother and turned to berate "her son" as a possible easy target. When he saw me, though, he yelped and dropped his stick. He fell into a swift bow.

"My apologies, y-your lordship. I didn't know that you was interested in wyverns and…er…any beast you want is—"

"Enough." I dismissed his antics with a wave of my hand. "As my mother said, we have no interest in any of your creatures. We merely wish to purchase transportation."

"O-of course, your lordship, your ladyship. Please, right this way. We'll get you where you need to go!" The man scrambled off, not even checking to see that we were following him.

"Would you care to explain that?" Mother asked.

"I told you. I'm Death's heir. My power is…not inconsiderable." In a past lifetime, I would have flinched away from acknowledging such power. Now, though, I knew it was merely a part of me. And that part of me scared a great many people. "I'm known around these parts. When we travel north, the reaction should not be quite so extreme."

She stared at me. The sort of scrutiny that children feared, the one that was a mix of confusion and shock, just edging on the verge of disappointment. I shifted the weight of my rucksack and followed after the wyvern keeper, climbing into one of the saddles and strapping in. My mother followed, silent.

Wyvern travel wasn't particularly comfortable.

We were sitting on the back of large, winged creatures, and they invariably moved when they launched into the air and flew. My first trip on a wyvern, I'd nearly been sick. Since then, I had grown used to the unfortunate means of travel, and while I would never like it, I at least wasn't nauseous.

"Whoever came up with this deserves a swift kick to the head," Mother snarled, hunched over, head between her knees. I patted her back and received a glare in return.

We travelled for about two hours before the wyvern let us off at the edge of the Northern Reaches. My mother collapsed as soon as we reached solid ground, and the wyvern keeper bowed several times before turning to tend to his beast. I took a few minutes to orient myself and look around.

The Northern Reaches were full of hills that spawned from the mountains to the west, where Yolanda's people lived. The hills here weren't nearly so tall or treacherous, and they were deceptive in their lush appearance. They had grasses and trees covering their surface, giving the impression of gentleness. I knew, though, that there lurked some decidedly nasty beings in their valleys.

"Well, well, fancy meeting you here."

I spun around. Standing at the edge of the wyvern station was a person I knew well. Small, lithe, with blue-grey skin, white hair tied in a long braid, wearing black leather and far more weapons than should have fit on any one person. Neja, the djinn, and my girlfriend.

I rushed to her, wrapping my arms around her and avoiding as many of the pointy ends of her weapons as I could. It was an acquired talent, one I'd picked up very quickly when hugging the be-weaponed djinn became my daily ritual. "What are you doing here?" I asked.

Neja squeezed me back, then pulled away. "I got a text from Baz. It sounded important, so I caught a ride with a local caravan. I wasn't too far away, anyways."

I felt the familiar squeeze in my chest when I was with her, something that hadn't changed at all since losing my humanity. "Thank you."

Neja waved off my thanks, looking around. "Always, Cal. Not to mention I couldn't pass up the opportunity to meet your *mother*."

Ah. Oh. Whoops. In my excitement to see Neja again, I had forgotten about my mother. And that Neja being here meant the two would meet. Swallowing a wince, I turned. Mother was now sitting on a rock, looking miserable. Judging by the pallor of her skin, she was feeling a bit better—at least, she wasn't green anymore—but it would probably be some time before we could venture forth.

Before I could say something, my girlfriend

marched past me towards Mother. She stopped feet from where Mother sat. With all the dignity that a proud British woman could muster, my mother raised her head, looked Neja over with a critical eye, and said, "Can I help you?"

"Yes. I'm Neja. Your son's partner."

"I wasn't aware that being Death's heir required a partnership," Mother said drily. I winced and moved to step in. Neja got there first.

"Girlfriend," she said. "Partner as in girlfriend. We sleep together."

I choked.

Mother made a humming sound. "I see. Calvin? When were you going to tell me about this?"

Never. My terrifying mother and girlfriend-with-many-weapons in the same place? At the same time? Yeah, it was definitely a situation to avoid.

"Mother, meet Neja. Neja, my mother, Teresa Thorpe. She's apparently the last Knight, and dragons are trying to kill her, so she's going on a quest with me as I go through the dragon lands to, er, sort things out." I looked around, tugging at the collar of my shirt. "I wonder if there's a place that sells coffee around here."

Neja burst out laughing. "Your face! Stars and stones, Cal, it's not that bad."

"He always did have a penchant for overreaction,"

Mother agreed. "Now, introductions aside, we need to figure out where we're going."

"That way." I gestured vaguely north. Neja sighed.

"It's a three-day hike across the Northern Reaches, Cal. You're going to want to hire transportation."

"Where?" I waved my hands at the empty landscape. "I don't see any horse sellers."

"There's a village not far from here. Come on, you great oaf." Neja wrapped my hand in hers and tugged me along. I very nearly turned to my mother for help and decided against it. She was already standing, brushing herself off and striding alongside Neja with the determination that sent shivers down the backs of all my teachers when it was time for a conference.

We hiked about an hour through the hills. Neja found some ridiculous game trail that cut directly up one hill and down another, which had my muscles burning by the time we reached the halfway point to this village. I wheezed, propping my hands on my knees. I was supposed to be some sort of heir to an eldritch force of the universe, the inevitable ending, and I couldn't even hike without losing my breath.

Surely there was some sort of irony in that.

Mother, on the other hand, was perfectly fine, taking in the sights around us with interest, completely unaffected by the strenuous hike, despite the fact that her shoes looked brand new. She and Neja had been chatting for the last half-hour, talking about me, discussing each other's work, talking about me. Mother seemed to be a little confused by Neja, or perhaps by her interest in me. She was a badass bounty hunter djinn, and I was, well, let's just say that upon first inspection, I was hardly terrifying.

I was musing the distinct oddity of my current situation while resting against a tree, trying to catch my breath, when the inevitable happened. Things went wrong.

A figure dressed in what looked like poorly tanned animal skins jumped out. He was probably human—mostly—with skin browned by the sun, a dark gold beard that was more mat than hair, and a wicked-looking scimitar. Which he pointed at my throat.

"Come with me, or die," he snarled, jabbing me just enough with his knife to draw blood.

I sighed. "I really don't want to get into this right now."

"Oh, is this *inconvenient* for you? Should I come back later?" the man sneered. Great, a sarcastic robber.

"Get away from my son." The words were spoken calmly, as if ordering a drink at a coffee shop, but one look at Mother made it very clear she meant business. Without my noticing, she had drawn her sword and now held it expertly before her, as though she'd done this before.

The robber, though, simply scoffed. "Yeah? What's he worth to you?"

"Teresa, perhaps you'd better let Cal handle this," Neja said, though she had a hand on one of the daggers at her belt. "He is more capable than—"

"No. I don't care how capable he is, no one threatens my son before my very eyes and gets away with it." Mother twisted her sword in a dance and lunged. I half-expected the robber to slice my throat by accident as he stumbled backwards, but I managed to escape with only a mild cut. The robber, on the other hand, was severely outmatched. He fended off my mother's attack with increasing desperation, eventually tripping over a protruding tree root and falling to the ground.

My mother took his hand off at the wrist.

Over his screams, she said, quite clearly, "I am Teresa Thorpe, last of the Knights, and I will not tolerate threats to my own. Do you understand me?"

The robber nodded frantically, scrambling away. He turned tail and ran.

I was tempted to stare at Mother, at the blood now splattering her clothes, at the look of righteous fury on her face, at the sword in her hand. Instead, I leaned against the tree again and groaned.

"Mother," I said. "That was not good."

"What? He was going to kill you. Cutting off his hand seemed a fair payment." She cleaned her sword on the edge of her jacket and sheathed it again, all in one fluid movement. She'd done this sort of thing before.

"While it is eminently disturbing to see you engaged in acts of violence, that is not what I meant." I removed my glasses and rubbed my eyes. "First off, I am impossible to kill. Literally. Second, you just announced to the entire lands bordering the home of the dragons that the Knight they've been searching for is here."

Mother frowned. "Oh. I see."

"What's a quest without a little danger?" Neja asked, grinning with more teeth than was strictly necessary. "Come on, the village is just over this hill."

CHAPTER 4

The village was less a neat array of cottages and shops that you might find in some of the more established areas of Elsewhere, and a bit more of a collection of people who were obviously trying to evade the law and had simply ended up in the same place. In other words: it was a mess.

The houses were little more than boards and logs held together with hope and mud. The streets were simply worn down with the passage of people, leaving uneven divots and holes of mud that one had to hop over on a regular basis. There was one established building in the whole spot and it seemed to serve as both tavern and market. I saw wares being advertised on tables right next to where people would eat and drink, resulting in some very fragrant items for purchase.

My mother scowled at a child who tried to pick her pocket. The child, sensibly, ran away.

"I wouldn't call this a village," I told Neja.

"A shanty town, perhaps," Mother agreed. She shook a bit of muck off her shoe. "If that."

"Admittedly, it's not the most reputable spot." Neja sidestepped a drunk who stumbled into the mud face first. "But they will sell what we need."

"I don't see any horses." If a horse had been to this desolate pit, then I'd eat my hat. If I had a hat.

"We're not looking for horses." Neja turned a corner and nodded, hands on her hips. "This is the spot."

This was perhaps the second edifice I'd actually call a building. It had no real signage out front—not that I imagined people in this place read much—and the windows were all covered over with some sort of cloth. Still, it seemed like there was a reasonably steady stream of people in and out, the ones coming out looking far more pleased with life than the ones going in.

"A brothel?" Mother clucked her tongue in distaste. "What are we going to find at a brothel that can transport us across the Northern Reaches?"

Even as she said that, I heard a horrible screeching sound from behind the brothel. I winced. "Not lindworms. Please. Or any other wyrm variant."

"You'll just have to wait and see." Neja linked her arm with mine and we went into the brothel.

It was precisely what one would expect from a brothel in a shantytown on the edge of the Northern Reaches. That is, the walls were wood, the decor was colourful and gaudy, and there were half-dressed people of various races strewn about on couches and cushions. Some were obviously drunk. Others were engaged in foreplay. It was, in other words, a mess of noise and colour and activity, all of which I found to be too loud.

Neja pulled me through the mess of people to a desk that looked like a hotelier's reception desk, complete with concierge. He was a dark-skinned human of some sort, though the vertical slits for eyes spoke to a different sort of ancestor. He wore a red suit and cap and smiled politely at us. "Welcome to the Golden Flower. My name is Raj. How may I assist you?"

"Hello, Raj. We need to hire some transportation." Neja flashed him a flirtatious smile. The concierge looked flustered, either by the number of visible weapons Neja carried, or her good looks. Either way, I was not going to interfere in her machinations.

"Destination?" Raj opened a ledger and started flipping through pages.

"The dragon lands," my mother said.

The concierge spluttered, knocking his pen and ink across the page and ruining the ledger. He turned a ghastly shade or orange, revealing some subtle spots to his skin. "A thousand apologies! I was startled; not one traveller who has ventured to the dragon lands has returned. It has become, hmm, taboo."

Neja flashed that smile again. "I think the dragons will make an exception for us."

If they didn't, then there would be trouble. Mostly for us, but I was willing to be Mother would dole out just as much as she got. Neja, too. Me? I was resigned to my fate either way.

"Certainly," Raj said, bowing slightly at the waist. "However, given the, ah, danger, I must insist that any transport be purchased outright." Then he listed a price that had Neja coughing, me sighing, and my mother looking thoroughly confused.

I handed over the business credit card. "Charge it to me."

"Very good, sir."

A few signatures on some paperwork, some furtive glances thrown at us by the concierge, and we were ushered quickly out the back of the building to a pen full of…ostriches.

"You're kidding me." I folded my arms and scowled, just so Neja would know I was serious.

"Relax, Cal. They're perfectly rideable. Bigger

than your mortal realm beasts. They can run really fast, too."

"They also bite," Mother pointed out. "Well, at least they're not camels. Camels smell absolutely revolting, and they spit."

With that, we were led to three ostriches, saddled and ready to go. They were larger than their mortal realm cousins, towering above my head by a good foot. Their feathers were also jet black. My steed gave me the side-eye and let out that screeching sound that was somewhere beyond the realm of furious goose.

"Why couldn't we buy horses?" I asked Neja as she helped me clamber into the saddle. My ostrich squawked indignantly as I pulled on some feathers, flaring his wings and buffeting me in the head.

"Horses are too valuable up here. Some of the local hill dwelling goblins use them for meat. There are warbands, too, that will steal any horse they can find. Ostriches, as you can see, are able to defend themselves. That, and it makes more sense to keep them alive for their eggs than it does to kill them for meat."

Curse her logic.

I managed to get into the saddle with only one more buffet from the stupid bird's wings. Mother was already saddled and had her bird under control. Neja, too, hopped into the saddle of her bird managed it expertly, practically dancing rings around me.

"Ready?" Neja asked.

"No," I grumbled.

"Proceed," Mother said.

Neja gave a whoop, tightened her hands on the reins, and tapped her heels into the sides of her ostrich. The bird jerked into motion, mine and Mother's following quickly afterwards.

Ostriches, in case you weren't aware, are really fast. They have those long legs to run from just about any predator they might encounter, and they know how to use them. They kick, they bite, and they run. As such, I held on for dear, well, not life that's certain, and within moments, we were away from the village and off into the Northern Reaches.

After the first burst of speed, the ostriches slowed to a reasonable trot, not struggling at all with our weight. They followed Neja's lead without question, taking game trails with ease that would have had me tripping and falling quite dramatically. Once I got the hang of balancing on the back of a giant bird, I began to relax. I wouldn't call it enjoyable, per se, as my muscles were protesting loudly, but it was hardly the worst trip I've ever taken.

The hills became more dramatic as we went on, not necessarily in height, but in sheer impressive stature. They were broader, the vegetation lusher.

There were rocks strewn about the landscape that looked as though they'd been flung there—a possibility, if there were giants in the region—or, more likely, they'd fallen in a landslide. It was the sort of landscape that made one feel quite small.

It was also, as I soon discovered, the perfect landscape for ambushes.

We rounded the corner of one valley just as the sun was entering the golden hour. Neja had been searching for a viable camp site for about an hour, now, and was having no luck. Not that there weren't spots we could have bedded down, but she deemed all poorly defensible. Mother was beginning to grouse, I was quite sore, and even Neja began to look weary.

A rock clattered from above, skittering onto the ground before us. Neja yanked on the reins of her ostrich, who gave an indignant honk. My bird stopped almost immediately. He ruffled his feathers and hissed.

"Dismount," Neja ordered. We obeyed.

Moments later, a band of goblins descended on us from above. Green skin, pointed ears, large, bulbous eyes, teeth suitable for tearing. They wore patchwork armour and bore various pointed weapons: swords, an axe, a mace. We were quite thoroughly surrounded.

"Now, now, what have we here?" one of the

goblins asked, slinking forwards to sniff at us. "A group of people moving fast through the Northern Reaches. Suspicious, I call it."

"Hardly," Neja drawled. "Travellers to the Bog come through here all the time."

"The Bog is to the west. You are travelling directly north." The goblin ran a claw-tipped finger along the edge of their sword. They grinned, showing off those teeth and releasing quite the stench along the way. Mother made a face. I tried not to gag.

"Let us be on our way," Mother said in her best obey-or-die voice. "We won't harm you."

"I think you'll find you need to worry more about whether *we* will harm *you*." The goblin sneered at us. Their compatriots chuckled, rattling the sabres, as it were. They inched closer. Mother's ostrich hissed and lunged, biting one of the more enthusiastic goblins on the ear. They wailed and withdrew.

"I hate ostriches," one of the smaller goblins grumbled, hefting their axe.

"Don't harm the birds, you idiot," the lead goblin snarled.

"What would it take for you to let us go on our way?" I asked, since Neja and Mother weren't getting anywhere with intimidation.

"Your bones in our stew, that's what."

I pushed my glasses up my nose. "Barring us

becoming dinner, what would it take?"

The goblin grunted. The others exchanged glances, as if not used to negotiating with their potential victims. "I fear that there is nothing you can offer us, foolish man," the lead goblin said, leering. "We have no need for gold except what we steal, and our bellies are empty."

As one, the goblins raised their blades. Neja drew a pair of daggers, ready to throw. Mother pulled out her sword. Me? Well, I let the world fall into shades of grey. Around me, I saw the pulsating yellow auras of everyone's lifeforce. Bright and golden-orange for Neja. Slightly worn and shot with copper for my mother. The goblins were all a sickly, neon yellow.

And me?

I glanced down at my hands and saw only the shadows of the void. The shadows of Death.

"I would prefer this didn't get messy," I said, an echo in my voice that hinted at what I was to become. The goblins either didn't notice or didn't understand, because moments later, they attacked.

Neja threw her daggers, each one landing in the eye of a goblin. She had drawn more weapons before her opponents could fall to the ground. Each movement was lethal, a dance that inevitably ended with her victory.

Mother wielded her sword with similar effect, though she aimed for limbs and chest rather than head or eye. Incapacitated, her opponents hissed and screamed and scurried away. She wasn't as graceful as Neja, but she certainly appeared capable.

The lead goblin, perhaps because of my perceived insolence in trying to bribe them, moved for me. They had a vicious gleam in their eye and attacked without hesitation or fear. They should have feared. The sword they bore whistled by my ear, a warning strike to make me flinch or to make me cower. I did neither. Instead, locking eyes with my opponent, I reached out and put my hands on their face.

Instantly, my Reaper magic as well as the magic of Death that beat within my chest latched onto the goblin's lifeforce. They gasped, eyes widening. I pulled. The lifeforce gave. In an instant, a blink, they were separated from their lifeforce. The goblin fell to the ground, dead.

Immediately, silence fell. The ones still fighting Neja and Mother froze, eyes fixated on me.

"Now," I said, wiping my hands on my trousers. "Perhaps we can renegotiate safe passage?"

The goblins didn't hesitate. They grabbed their weapons—and the weapons of their dead—then scurried back into the hills, scattering rocks and scree in their wake. Within moments, they were gone.

"Show off," Neja said, remounting her ostrich. "Come on, let's find someplace to camp."

CHAPTER 5

We sheltered in a slight divot in the side of one of the mountains, protected by an overhang of rock and some scrubby bushes. Neja made a small fire and we ate trail rations. My mother sniffed at the protein bar and took a dainty bite, her displeasure showing quite loudly.

"I've seen you do that before," Mother commented, washing down the meal with a mouthful of water. She grimaced at that, too, likely wishing it were wine. Personally, I'd have done a great many things for a decent cup of coffee.

"What?" I asked, eyeing the lizard that Neja turned on a spit over the fire. I decided to take my chances with the protein bar.

"Take something's life with a touch."

I frowned. Ah, yes. When I'd first returned to Mother after having worked for Death—ostensibly so I could help fix an unfortunate situation that Baz had caused—the house had been attacked by a smallish monster of some sort. I'd killed it in self defence in much the same way as I'd killed the goblin. Mother and Baz had both been shocked. Horrified, even, though they managed to hide that particular emotion well. I'd only recently awoken my Reaper abilities at that point and was barely in control of them.

Now? I imagined it was something quite different.

"It does come with the territory," I pointed out. "Being Death's heir and all, not to mention that I'm still a Reaper."

"Is it an easy thing?" she asked, still frowning over the wrapper of her protein bar. "To kill with your touch? To throw away life so easily?"

Something dark and dangerous rose up in me. My voice was cold, immortal. "I do not *throw* lives away. Death is an inevitability. It comes to all things. That goblin was offered a chance to negotiate a different path and chose otherwise."

"So it's not your fault?" Her words were accusatory, her expression inching towards a sneer. The part of me that remembered being human, remembered deferring to her, flinched.

"I did not say that. I said only that it could have been avoided had the goblin chosen otherwise. And, if you will recall, that one death meant the others chose to live."

She sniffed disdainfully. "I see. So easily justified, it must be the right thing."

"I did not say that either." I was practically growling, shadows gathering at my fingers. "Death is not right. Nor wrong. It merely is. The circumstances which surround it, surround *me*, happen while hearts still beat, while life still flows. Perhaps you should ask whether Life is right or wrong, that it brings so many to their end at my hands."

"Cal." Neja put a hand on my arm. The shadows immediately dissipated, though I still felt the coldness of the eternal void pumping through my veins. Like the space between stars, visible only through their brilliance. I took a breath and turned my thoughts away from endings and inevitability. Coffee. A good book. A pleasant fire.

After a few minutes, I opened my eyes. The fire crackled merrily before me. Neja continued to turn her lizard on its spit, though I could tell that it was starting to char. She kept watch on me, though, her movements designed to display the semblance of normality. She was ready to strike at a moment's notice.

Abruptly, I stood. "If you'll excuse me, I'm going

to see if there's some water nearby. Refill the canteens."

Without another word from my mother, who nodded imperiously, or Neja, who just smiled sadly, I slipped into the night.

I had always had poor night vision, even before being fitted with enormous glasses as a child, but away from the fire I found that the landscape was almost luminous. The light came from some source on the horizon, like the glow of a city. I didn't think it was a city, not given that the shantytown we'd passed through was considered civilisation for this part of the north.

I followed the glow for a bit, angling my path downwards to the valley floor. Water always seemed to gather in the low places, and I had to give some verisimilitude to my story, even if I had forgotten the canteens. I stumbled over loose rock and steadied myself on a few of the scrubby bushes. Finally, I tripped over a piece of dead tree and nearly fell into a small stream.

Water. Good. I bent my head to drink and was brought short by a hissing sort of laugh.

"I wouldn't drink that, if I were you." The voice was male, deep and quiet. Vast. "Not unless you enjoy having your innards turned to acid as you stand there."

"I've probably had worse," I said, but dutifully

stepped back from the stream. "What poisons the water?"

"The same thing that poisons this entire region. Runoff from the fires." The creature shifted and I saw a shape in the faint glow. It was about the size of a horse, with long neck, wings, a tail that dragged on the ground, and a triangular head with one horn wrapping around on the right and a broken stump on the left. Dragon. I needed to warn Mother.

"What fires?" I tried looking around, as if searching for these fires, but couldn't find my path in the dark. I'd wandered too far from my own campfire to see that, either.

"Those." The dragon nodded his head towards the glow in the distance. "You can only see them at night from this distance, but they burn constantly, and have done for centuries. Dragonfire. Those fools used it to mark the border of their lands, thinking that intimidation was the best method of keeping people away. They did not realise the consequences."

"They?" Surely he realised he was a dragon. Then again, I didn't want to assume. "You're a dragon. That makes it your lands, too."

"Do you claim all killers as priests of your order, Deathling?" the dragon asked. "No, I thought not. Just so, I may be a dragon, but those lands are not mine. They have not been for a very long time."

I'd met a dragon, once, and that but briefly. It had

traversed the realms to steal back a trove of eggs that —accidentally—ended up in my possession. I'd kept them safe, had returned them happily, and the dragon's voice still tried to tear me to pieces, still struck me with such fear that I could barely move. Only my mother, a Knight, could stand up to the dragon.

And now they wanted to kill her.

"Why doesn't your voice…" I trailed off, not knowing quite how to ask. Not knowing why I wanted to ask. I should have been running to Mother, not talking with her sworn enemy. Yet there I stood, hands in my pockets, studying as much of the dragon as I could see in the dark.

"Burn your mind?" The dragon chuckled, the sound like rocks grating together. "Partly because of what you are, for even we will eventually bow to Death. But mostly because, as I said, the others are far more fond of using intimidation as a display of power. They want the world, all the realms, to fear them. To cower at the mere sight of their claws. They want people to tremble in their presence, unable to stand to their might. It is a poor substitute for real power, and a tiresome one at that."

"I have seen a dragon cross realms," I said. "Is that not power?"

"The fae cross realms. As do any who go to the Goblin Market. Is their power any less?"

"You would have me believe that, what, dragons

are all bluffing?" I thought of the storm that spawned over my mother's house, the lightning that struck the stoop. There were legends of the dragons and their immense power. People feared them.

This dragon snorted, shaking his head, sparks trailing from his mouth. "There are magics inherent to the dragons, yes, but is that power?"

Oh, good, we were going to get metaphorical now. "What is it, exactly, that you want from me?"

"Want from you? Nothing. I merely sought to warn you of the stream's toxicity. It has been a long time since I have had any to talk with. I suppose it was nice. A change. However, if you wish, I will leave." He began to do just that, turning, his tail dragging in the dirt, wings limp at his side.

I groaned inwardly. "Wait."

He paused, head tilting.

"What should I call you?"

"Names have power, as you surely well know, Deathling. But, for the sake of politeness, you may call me Casperion."

"I'm Cal." I bowed, some instinct in me telling me what to do. "And, for fear of being considered incredibly stupid, what, exactly, were you trying to say about the other dragons?"

Casperion flashed his teeth, spots of white in the darkness. A smile, I gathered. "Not stupidity, but ignorance. Often mistaken for the same things. As to the others, well, they surround their lands in fire and instil fear in any who hear them speak. Why?"

"To be feared?"

"Just so. And if people fear you, they do not question."

I thought of Mother, who questioned everything, including her own son. No wonder the dragons wanted her dead. "Why are you telling me this?"

"Because you travel to the dragon lands, and because you are touched by Death. They will try to make you cower, and Death should cower before no one. And, perhaps, because I have been away from them too long and wish them to know the truth of the world."

Away from them. He'd been exiled, I was sure of it. There was a spark of a vendetta in his tone, a coldness. He wanted them to see what they'd done to him, and if that meant sharing their secrets, then he would do so, gladly. I shivered.

"What do you intend for them?" I asked bluntly. Casperion flashed his teeth again, no longer smiling.

"A great many things."

I considered. Mother would have a fit, if she deigned to be so emotionally involved. Neja certainly would be emotionally involved, but she'd be more likely to see the benefit of such an ally. Still, it wasn't my decision alone to make. I would have to ask the others.

I turned to tell Casperion that when I spotted a glint of metal in the darkness, barely illuminated by the distant light of the dragon fires. It was moving directly for the dragon. Without thinking, I leaped in front of the blade. It was a sword, heavy and familiar. And my mother, unused to swordcraft after all these years, couldn't turn it away in time. It cleaved into my chest with ease, splitting bone and lodging into my lungs.

I saw, for a brief moment, my mother's horrified expression before the world flared white and I died. When I woke again, my mother had pulled the sword from me and was now facing down Casperion, who reared up on his back legs, wings flaring, sparks trailing from his maw.

"Cal!" Neja said, pulling me to my feet. She winced at the ragged remains of my jumper. "I know you just died and all, but you may want to intervene."

"That was on my to-do list," I grumbled, rubbing my chest. I hated dying; it was always such a waste of good clothes, and sometimes the pain lingered. Just because I couldn't be killed didn't mean I felt no pain. Ignoring this, I lurched towards Mother, managing to stumble into her just as she lunged for Casperion.

"Enough!" I snapped as her sword went for me again. "Stop stabbing me!"

"Cal?" she asked, uncertain. She must have figured things out fairly quickly, because in an instant, she was back in a guarded pose, her sword pointed at the dragon. "Get out of the way."

"No."

Mother narrowed her eyes at me. "You would interfere in the natural order of things?"

"I do so all the time. Now put down the sword and we can all have a nice, civilised conversation." I glared at her.

"Dragons don't have civilised conversations," she snarled, but either because I was in the way or she decided to listen to me, she lowered the point of her blade towards the ground. In turn, Casperion dropped to the ground and furled his wings.

"A Knight," he said, tone somewhere between shock and dismay. "I thought your kind had died out long ago. No wonder the others have been…on edge, lately."

"I thought you hadn't had contact with the others for centuries," I accused. Casperion nodded.

"I can still see, Deathling. I am not so old as to be blind. Any fool could see that they are agitated. Sending out members of their ilk across realms who have not ventured forth before, or who are desperate to prove themselves. Dragons, as a general rule, do not leave their lands, even across realms, unless there is something quite pressing to be dealt with. A Knight would certainly fall into that category."

My mother gaped at me, incredulous. Neja came up beside me and studied the smallish dragon, hands quite clearly on her weapons belt. "You're not going to kill her?" she asked, jerking her head towards Mother.

"I have no interest in killing a Knight," Casperion said smoothly. "Too messy. The metaphysical repercussions are always such a bother."

"Mother?" I asked pointedly.

She pursed her lips, then nodded and sheathed her sword. "I have no personal vendetta with the dragon. If he does not attack me or mine, then I shall do the same."

Casperion blinked, rearing his head back. "How unusual! A Knight who puts down the sword for no other reason than she was asked. And your mother, as well, Deathling? Well, I do believe we should have a further conversation, Lady Knight. Would any of you care for some tea? I have a decent selection back at my den."

"You wouldn't happen to have any coffee, would you?" I asked, perhaps more hopefully than was polite.

Neja elbowed me in the gut. "We'd be thrilled. Lead the way!"

CHAPTER 6

About an hour later, after collecting the ostriches—who were less than thrilled about Casperion, but did as Mother told them—and walking through the darkness to his den, we were seated beside a cozy fireplace, tea in hand. A dragon's den, to be honest, looked nothing like what I expected. I had thought of piles of gold or jewels or whatever else dragons hoarded, but this place looked more like Death's mansion than anything. Wood panelling, dark rugs, tasteful decor. Granted, everything was sized for a dragon, but it was still remarkably comfortable.

Despite the lack of coffee.

"Why would you even *consider* allying yourself with me?" Mother had wasted no time getting Casperion's story about the fearful nature of the other dragons out of him and was now well into the berating him about motives part of the conversation. Neja and I listened politely, but were more focused on our tea.

"Why do you consider yourself to be my natural enemy?" the dragon returned easily. "Knights and dragons are opposing forces, perhaps, but that does not necessarily mean we are enemies. Life and Death are opposites, yet they are married. Day and night. Fire and water. Opposite, yes, but not necessarily adversarial. Admittedly, Knights and dragons have stood against each other for many generations, but it is not a universal truth."

Mother frowned and sipped her tea. She looked less than convinced. "Why, then, are we opposites? You seem polite, even-tempered, open to reason. As, I would hope, am I."

Here, Casperion's easy smile faltered slightly. He set his over-large cup on the side table and read-justed his wings behind him. "In the beginning, dragons were, shall we say, apex predators. We had magic at our disposal in a world—just the one at the time—where magic was not ubiquitous. Larger, stronger, and more intelligent than every other race except perhaps the gods, there were few who dared stand against us. The natural consequence of such things is that power was given to us with ease. It became expected, and therefore, abused. Then, the first Knights appeared.

"We didn't know if they were imbued with magic by someone, or if it was a natural development, only that they were able to stand against us. Perhaps not with ease, as we were still larger and more powerful, but with surety. Our voices had no effect on them. Our magic was dulled in their presence. They seemed to see through our armour to a singular weakness and were able to slay us when before we had never been killed. Over time, the magic in Knight blood became more concentrated, as did certain traits. Self-righteousness. Heroism. Chivalry."

Casperion sighed, shuddering dramatically. "Even after the realms were separated, there was no stopping the force of chivalry from crossing the barrier. Quite a bother. The Fae still seem to follow those rules, though of course, they have twisted them to their own devices, as they are wont to do."

"Ahem." Neja coughed into her tea. Casperion blinked, looking at us with mild confusion.

"Oh, I do apologise. I quite diverged from the question. Let's see. Why dragons and Knights are adversarial." He hummed, more than a few sparks spitting from his mouth at the sound. "It all comes down to one simple thing: power. The dragons were accustomed to all-encompassing power. Only a few beings could ever oppose us, and so we expected blind obedience, loyalty, slavery even. Awe. Terror. The Knights, on the other hand, were sworn to defend the weak amongst their kind—humans, mostly, though there was a dwarf once who...I digress again. Knights gave people their power back. Defended those who had none. They took from the dragons. We didn't much like that. And such, a rivalry was born. No matter that the Knights could easily have worked with us had our power been divested properly, as true power should be."

I let my mind wander as the dragon meandered on about the nature of power. My mother seemed fascinated and brought up several points of philosophy which escaped me entirely. Neja seemed more inclined to nap, dozing in a chair that nearly swallowed her small frame, face illuminated by the fire.

"What do you know of the Fisher King?" I asked, interrupting Casperion as he was discussing the various genealogies of prominent Knight families.

The amiable, conversational dragon vanished in an instant. Fire bloomed in his eyes and he bared his teeth. "Why do you ask, Deathling?" he growled, the sound rumbling in his throat. I met his gaze evenly; as he'd said before, I didn't need to cower before a dragon just because they were large and powerful. I was a Reaper. I had Death's own heart beating in my chest. I would become Death someday. There was little this creature could do to harm me.

So I waited, saying nothing.

"I know what the human legends say of the Fisher King. That he holds the cup, waiting for someone virtuous to ask the right question, to save his land. That he rules over a dead kingdom, guarding the answer to everlasting life—eternal power—for the day his lands are saved." Casperion scoffed at this, the sound more a snarl than a laugh. "Shadows of the original story. Cobbled together and changed over the years when combined with religious stories and creative storytellers. Such as all legends are distorted."

"Tell me of the Fisher King," I said, this time a command.

Casperion regarded me archly, that same fire in his eyes flickering the longer he held my gaze. The room seemed to fade away until Mother, Neja, the warm surroundings disappeared into mist and shadow. I knew without asking that I was in a realm of the mind—his or mine, I didn't know—and that no one else could hear us or would know we had gone.

"The Fisher King is a blight." Casperion tossed his head, now crowned with two full horns instead of the broken pair. Behind him, his wings stretched fully, broad and strong instead of the weak things I realised he bore in the real world. This was him as he had been, once long ago.

"A literal blight? Like with crops?" I surreptitiously looked at my hand and, so far as I could tell, it was much the same as always. At least my mental image was accurate.

"Not as such, no. He—*it*—has a hunger. For life. For magic. For power. They say that a thousand memories ago, it arose from the edge of knowing and began devouring all in its path. Sometime later, it became sentient. Spoke. Lured its prey forth and gave power to a select few so that they might bring more to it. A demon, in a sense, hungering for anything that stands before it. It conquered most of the dragon lands before it was contained." Casperion rattled his scales. "No one knows how, only that it was contained to a patch of land beside a lake. The dragons settled the scorched places and used their vast magic to regrow and recreate a portion of what was lost. One of the few selfless things that they did."

"The Fisher King isn't dead, though," I mused. "Just bound."

"It still hungers. Any who wander in its path are taken. Devoured. Bound, somewhere in that impossible void that is its being. There are legends, rumours more like, that suggest those taken can be recovered by a virtuous hero. By one who knows no fear, who upholds right over wrong, who stands unblemished. The Fisher King cannot devour such a being and will disgorge all that it has eaten rather than face fate at this hero's hand. A foolish tale, even for the magic of Elsewhere, but it's likely where the human legends were born."

I was certain that I was not the virtuous hero. I'd killed. I was far from selfless. Sure, I had my good moments, and I really, really hated bullies, but I was human. I closed my eyes. I *had been* human. Now, I didn't know.

"I have to find the Fisher King," I said after a moment, keeping my eyes closed. I could feel Casperion's interest like a brand upon my skin.

"Why? It is certain death." He paused. "Perhaps even for one such as you."

"Then I die." And I would, too. Everything died. I knew that. In the deepest part of my soul, I knew that. Death himself was dying because of me. One day, I would likely die because of someone else. Perhaps now was that day. Maybe I could save the Reapers before I did die, though. They deserved that I try.

"You are a strange creature. You reek of self-preservation, of comfortable living. Yet...here you are, asking about your own doom." Casperion flared those perfect wings. "Not a Knight in truth, perhaps, but you certainly have all the signs of having been raised by one."

The dragon drew his head close to mine; I could smell sulfur and brimstone on his breath. In a low growl, he said, "I will make you a deal, Deathling."

"I'm listening."

"Bring me with you on your journey through the dragon lands, and swear that the Knight will not harm me, and I will lead you to the Fisher King."

A reasonable request, except for the bit about my mother not harming him. I couldn't promise that, not on her behalf. She would flay me if I did. But a guide to both the dragon lands and the Fisher King would be…useful, to say the least.

"I will bring you with us, and I will swear to stand between you and her if she deems harm necessary. No more than that can I promise."

The dragon snorted, blowing sparks. The mist began to fade. "Bargained and done, it is sworn."

I felt the magic of the bargain lay itself over my shoulders, as usually happened with these things. The mist and shadow fell away to be replaced with fire and wood panelling and tea. Neja and Mother blinked, looking between Casperion and myself as though waiting for an answer.

The dragon chuckled slightly. "Old minds such as mine do wander so. Now, we were talking about the journey to the dragon lands, were we not?"

Neja narrowed her eyes at me, but Mother, ignorant of the workings of Elsewhere and magic, just nodded her head. "I know you haven't been there for many years, but surely you can give us some information?"

Casperion bared his fangs. "Better than that, I can guide you. I am a poor story teller, and it is better to show you in person."

A poor story teller indeed. I muffled a snort. He'd been telling stories since I met him. Words poured from him like water from a fountain. He was, though, a poor liar. Even my mother began to frown, her keen mind picking up on the inconsistency.

Neja looked at me again, pointedly this time. I shook my head. Later. I would tell her later about the bargain.

"Why do you want to go back to a place that exiled you?" Mother asked coldly. "For that matter, why depend on us to take you back?"

Yep. One did not easily pull the wool over my mother's eyes. Certainly Baz had tried that enough in his youth. And just about every time he saw my mother.

Casperion rose from his chair, pacing before the fire. The den was dragon-sized, but with him pacing and the three of us sitting in close proximity, there was every chance of getting hit with a wing or a tail. But seeing him walk in the light, now, I could tell just how worn he was. His broken horn. His wings, stiff, the left one shredded at the edge. His tail with a severe kink at the tip. Scars along his hide, showing a break in the scales. This dragon was old. Worn. And he bore a fury that was palpable.

"That is the funny thing about exile as a dragon," he hissed. "Once gone, it is impossible to return unless brought back. Someone else must open the way for me, and none of the other dragons would ever deign to lower themselves to welcoming an *exile*. But, I am still a dragon. Everywhere else I go, I would be feared. People would run. Or demand that I protect them as a lord of ancient, as a being of power. I am not a god to be bent to the wills of others."

"That's why you're in this place," Neja realised aloud. She set her tea down with a clatter. "The northern reaches. There isn't much here for civilisation. You obviously like civilisation." She gestured to the trappings of the den. "So why would someone like you live here? In sight of the dragon lands, but so far from civilisation?"

Casperion snapped his tail on the ground in a *thwap*. "I have been away from the world too long if beings like you can see right through me. I admit, fully and freely, that I want to return to the life afforded dragons in our own territory. And that I want to see the others when they realise that I will not be forgotten."

Revenge.

The word lay unspoken between us. I knew that the others felt it. Tasted it. The want that Casperion had for revenge was overpowering. And I had promised to facilitate it by bringing him with us.

"We need a guide," I said to Mother and Neja. Mother frowned.

"We do not—"

"Yeah," Neja said, rubbing the back of her neck. "We really do."

"We are perfectly capable!" Mother snapped. "There's no need for this."

"You don't understand. The dragon lands are completely uncharted. We know that the Fisher King is north, but that's it. And the dragons aren't going to take too kindly to a Knight trespassing on their territory, no matter that she's accompanying Death's heir. A guide will help mitigate the chaos." Neja looked Casperion over, gaze critical. "You will not harm us."

"I wouldn't dream of it," the dragon said archly.

"Then we will bring you with us."

CHAPTER 7

The remainder of the journey through the northern reaches was uneventful, except for trying to control ostriches around a dragon. Casperion flew for short bursts, landing ahead of us while we navigated over hills and around obstacles. Then, once his wings were rested, he would leap back into the air and wait for us again some distance ahead. The ostriches weren't thrilled about the travelling companion. Understandable. My mother wasn't thrilled, either.

Finally, after another day of travel, Casperion stopped flying ahead. "I will walk from here so as not to rouse suspicion. Your birds will do you no good the closer we get to the dragon lands. They will baulk at the fire, if nothing else, but proximity to predators is likely to make them run."

After having paid an exorbitant price for the birds, and growing rather attached to my own feathered steed, I was reluctant to just leave them in the middle of nowhere, but nor were they in any fit state to do anything, just from being in close proximity to Casperion. Neja was the first to release her bird, slipping the saddle from its back and waving her arms at it to run off. It did so, gladly.

"They'll be better off on their own here, Cal," she said. "Goblins don't love ostriches because they bite and kick and run. They have better defences than most. And with three of them, they'll do well."

"Don't be sentimental," my mother said, following Neja's example. "They wouldn't give you the same courtesy."

I thought of my pet, Tempest, a ghostly miniature griffin who lived in my rooms back on Death's lands. She had died for me. Willingly. I would never underestimate the heart of animals. I stroked the neck of my ostrich and pulled off both saddle and bridle. Then, in an undertone, I said, "If you can make it to Death's lands, he will see to it you are taken care of."

The bird blinked, squawked, and ran off after its companions.

"Your heart will get you into trouble one day," Mother said.

"It'll be alright, Cal," Neja said, rubbing my arm.

Casperion watched all of this with a slight frown,

tail twitching. He said nothing, though, just turned and started towards the glow. It had grown brighter the closer we got, visible now even in the light of day. There was also a distinct increase in heat as we travelled forth; the vegetation that had grown in and on the hills started to be sparser, the leaves curled and dried at the edges. When we crested one last ridge, the vegetation was almost entirely dead, brown and shrivelled from the heat.

Then, we were faced with the fire.

It was a solid wall, perhaps fifteen feet high, made up solely of flame. Orange, red, white, yellow, occasionally even a bit of blue. There was nothing at the base to indicate that something was burning, meaning that it was magic. Not that I had enough water left in my flask to douse more than a campfire. This was more than just fire, though, magical or otherwise. It was a very, very clear signal that the keepers of this place did not want to be disturbed.

They couldn't have been more clear if they'd had a big, giant sign that said, "Keep Out or Die."

"Right," Neja said, staring up at the fire. "How do we get through?"

I had a feeling she wasn't asking for herself. Neja was a djinn, a being made from smoke and fire and wishes. As far as I knew, fire wouldn't harm her, even if it were magical. Me, well, I could walk right through the flame. It would hurt like the dickens, and I would definitely ruin my clothes, but I would live. Casperion could come through in my wake.

My mother, on the other hand, despite being a Knight, was fully human.

She would die.

"We knock, of course," Casperion said. With a breath, he reared back onto his hind legs, lifted his head, and roared.

The sound reverberated through the air and my bones, rattling both until I could feel nothing but trembling. It wasn't so much fear as a full understanding of the power of this dragon. It was the power of beings who could break the world with a thought. Posturing and fear or not, the dragons did possess power in spades.

I wondered whether Casperion was, in fact, a better liar than I thought. I wondered if I should have thought of that before. Probably.

The fire split for a moment, responding to the dragon's roar.

"Go, now, and take my claw." Casperion held out his paw to me. I held it, and we proceeded forwards. The fire's heat was enough to make my eyes water and then to evaporate that water. We kept going, me in the lead, Casperion hopping on three legs behind, Neja and my mother side by side.

In a blink and a rush of heat and magic, we were through the fire and face to face with paradise.

Stretching as far as I could see were lush rolling hills dotted with trees and fields, penned in by low stone walls. There were some cows grazing a ways off, and perched on a hill in the distance was a square stone tower and some low buildings. The air was crisp and pleasant, protected from the impossible heat at our backs. Birds chirped. The breeze blew pleasant flower scents in our direction.

It looked, to be honest, like the Italian countryside. To be more specific, it looked like the Italian countryside of the late 1400s, when I'd accidentally travelled back in time and met Machiavelli. (Incidentally, this was also when I lost my soul, but that's a different story.)

Once the thought took hold in my mind, it wouldn't let go. The hair and the back of my neck prickled and I shivered with discomfort. A quick check of Mother and Neja showed that they looked pleased with this place, that they didn't suspect anything out of the ordinary. And why would they? They hadn't come back in time with me. They'd never lived this particular memory of mine.

"What is this place?" I asked Casperion in a low voice.

He blinked at me, surprised. "You feel it? The way the land twists itself to suit you?"

"It's creepy." While I'd had some good times in Italy, I'd also lost a very good friend and come to terms with the unstable nature of Life and Death. "Why this place? This…memory?"

"Memory?" Neja asked, finally turning to me with a frown. "It's just a nice countryside."

"No." I shook my head. "It's not."

"The Deathling is right," Casperion said, adjusting his wings on his back and looking around with interest. "The nature of the dragon lands is such that it…bends to the presence of those with significant power. Normally, that would be the dragons. But with your entrance, well, things have changed."

Mother shifted the sword at her back so it was easier to draw. "What you're saying is that by coming here, Cal has essentially announced our presence to all the dragons?"

Casperion nodded. "You grasp the situation quite clearly."

He eyed me, smoke drifting from his nostrils. I'd disquieted him, somehow. Was it that I was more powerful than the dragons, that this place had changed to somewhere from my memories? Was it that I felt the magic of this place? I didn't know.

"So," Neja said, loosening a short sword from its hilt. "We wait?"

"There are certainly worse places to do that," Casperion agreed, looking around. "What is this place?"

"Italy," I said. "Late fifteenth century."

Just before I lost my soul and this entire sequence of events started. Back when I thought I was just Death's marketing agent. Things were so simple then. For a brief moment, I felt a stab of longing. It was gone just as fast. There was no need to mourn the past. Things were as they were, and I could not change what was done. Regret was a vestige of my humanity and useless to me now.

Still, I rubbed my chest until my heartbeat slowed.

"Well, if they were going to pluck a place out of your head, I suppose it could be worse," Mother said. "It's not that ridiculous shop where you worked as a teenager, though you and Baz certainly spent a lot of time there."

I sighed. Then, since I had no intention of waiting around for the dragons, I started off across the hills towards the tower. Neja was the first to run after me.

"Cal! Wait!" she said, catching up and threading her arm through mine. In a quieter voice, she said, "Are you alright?"

"Perfectly."

"It's just...you lost your humanity less than a month ago, and now you're considered the most powerful being in the dragon lands. Including the dragons." Neja squeezed my arm a bit. "Surely the change has to…"

"Shock me?" I shook my head. "Neja, my love, can you honestly say it's a surprise? I am to take over for Death. Sooner or later, I couldn't say, but it is inevitable. I already have his power in my blood, and the Reaper abilities besides. I'm…I'm not surprised that they consider me powerful."

She tugged at me until I looked at her. Bright eyes, wide with concern. Weapons readily within reach. A fragility about her that was once shared with me. Mortality. In that instant, I knew I would lose her. She would grow old and die, or be killed and die, or become ill and die. Her life was a candle, snuffed out with the ease of a single breath. I, on the other hand, was carved from diamond in comparison. Difficult to shape, harder to destroy.

I wanted to hold on to her. Desperately.

I knew, though, that she would slip through my grasp like smoke.

"Cal," Neja said, voice a low murmur as Casperion and my mother drew closer. "Not so long ago, you were aghast at being considered more than Death's marketing agent."

I closed my eyes for a brief moment. "I know."

"And now…?"

I smiled and tugged her along, continuing our ascent towards the tower and surrounding buildings. "What would you like me to say? That I wish I could go back to that life? That I wish I were nothing more than a marketing agent? It's done, Neja. Don't look at me like that. I'm still me, in essence."

She tilted her chin down, refusing to meet my gaze. "I know."

Her words felt like a lie, though I was certain I had spoken the truth.

"What is this?" Mother asked, finally catching us up. She frowned at the buildings before us. "That looks…"

"Like a pub," Casperion said, sounding thoroughly confused. I was a little surprised that the dragon knew what a pub was, but then again, he had served us tea from a proper tea service, so who was I to judge?

"I believe it's a tavern," Neja said, staring at it. "At least, it looks like a tavern."

I had taken a young, unknown Niccolo Machiavelli to a tavern once upon a time. I'd bet my glasses that this was the same place. I pushed through the door and was unsurprised by the interior. Dark wood, tile and dirt floor, the air of a busy, well-loved place. It was empty of people, which was the only difference between my memory and this place. I didn't hesitate, though, instead going straight to the barrel of beer and pouring a pint.

Even the beer tasted as I remembered.

Neja and Mother joined me at a table in the centre of the room, and Casperion wedged himself through the door, scraping down some of the wood with his scales. He growled in frustration.

"Maybe we should sit outside," Mother suggested.

"No, I can make it!" He shoved against the door and, using claw and scale, pushed himself inside, ruining the door and scraping away a good portion of the wall, as well. The dragon huffed and gave a shake before taking the offered pint of beer.

"This is horrible," he said, wrinkling his nose and pushing the alcohol away from him.

"Yep," I said, taking another sip. "Just like I remember."

"I think we need to have a conversation about what to expect from the other dragons," my mother said, pushing away her own pint without tasting it. She was a connoisseur of drink at the best of time and rarely bothered to drink beer. To have it proclaimed as horrible was enough to put her off entirely.

"Posturing," Casperion said with a huff. "They'll try to cow you, but it will be difficult to prove their superiority."

"Why?" Mother asked. "Certainly they had no such compunctions about attacking me on my doorstep in my own territory, that is, London. Here, we are in their territory."

"Look at the surroundings," Neja said, drinking heartily. "This is Cal's memory. Not the dragons.'"

"That's all well and good for you, Cal, but what about the rest of us?" Mother asked, folding her hands neatly on the table.

I tilted my head. There was a sound. Like the rumble of a thousand drums on the field of battle. Thunder in a storm that stretched from horizon to horizon. It was, I knew, the sound of the dragons flying towards us. "We're about to find out," I said, finishing off my beer.

I expected to go outside and meet the dragons, but it turns out there was no need. Before I could make a move for the door, the roof of the tavern was ripped off and replaced with the snarling head of a dragon big enough to blot out the sun. When faced with a creature like that, there really is only one thing to do.

"Afternoon!" I called. "I don't suppose you'd feel inclined to take us to your leader?"

CHAPTER 8

One thing I have learned in my time in Elsewhere is that creatures and people of all sorts, when faced with unerring politeness rather than immediate violence, will become immediately confused. The exception to this rule is the Fae, for whom politeness and violence are synonyms.

The giant dragon, therefore, did not immediately blast us with fire and burn us to a crisp. Instead, she made a small coughing sound and pulled back. "Oh, erm, yes, rather."

"Splendid!" I led my wary party to the door and we found ourselves outside the tavern, in the bucolic countryside, faced with about two dozen or so dragons of all sizes and colours. The largest was the one who had torn off the roof. The smallest was of a size with Casperion. They ranged from solid to a myriad of colours and had twisting horns or pointed horns or spikes on their tail or a veritable crown of pointed objects. They all, to a one, stared at me.

"I am leader here," a dragon of middling size said, hobbling forward. If I had thought Casperion old, then this dragon was truly ancient. Her scales were purple with a tinge of grey and white at the tips, the discolouration concentrated around her muzzle. Her wings were limp at her sides, the right one dragging on the ground. She had a missing tail and limped visibly. There was something in her look, though, that told me she could flatten us where we stood without more than a blink and a thought.

I decided to err on the side of caution and bowed at the waist, hand crossed at my chest. "Great Lady," I said, straightening. The dragon reared her head back, visibly confused. She sniffed, then frowned.

"Who are you? You smell of empty places and darkness, but there is only one who bears that scent and you are not he."

"I am his heir," I said, hiding a wince. Perhaps I should have had Death write a letter of introduction. That might have gone better than showing up unannounced. As it was, this news did not go over well with the dragons. They immediately broke out into conversation, growling and chuffing and talking over one another. Behind me, Casperion dug his claws into the earth, huffing in annoyance.

"Quiet!" the old dragon snapped, stomping her front feed on the ground. The others fell into silence. She extended her neck closer, narrowing her eyes at me. She sniffed once. Twice. Examined me in minute detail. "Why should I believe what you say? You who intrude on our lands, bringing two mortals and one who was exiled?"

My mother shifted so that her sword was loosened in its sheath. I eyed her to try and convey that this was Not The Time for such things, but anyone who has ever tried to force my mother into anything knows that a single look would do nothing. Neja, thankfully, put her hand on my mother's arm, keeping her still. For the moment.

"I was exiled on charges that were patently false and—"

The elder dragon bored her eyes into Casperion, who fell silent. "You were not invited to speak. I was addressing the supposed Heir to Death. Well, human, are you going to answer my question?"

Something in me rustled at her assumption that I was human, a power deep and terrible. She hissed and drew back. I slid my hands into my pockets and kept a relaxed posture so as to be non-threatening. "I don't particularly care whether you believe me. I am what I say I am and have no need to prove it to you.

However, if you require convincing, then look around you. Casperion told me that this place reflects a landscape from the most powerful around. To me, it looks like a corner of Italy that I visited. What does it look like to you?"

This caused another stir. The largest dragon snarled. "We should kill him for usurping our lands!"

I sighed. "I'm hardly usurping. I came here because—"

"How dare you threaten my son," Mother snarled in response. She shrugged Neja off and drew her sword, pointing it at the big dragon. The dragons all gasped at precisely the same time, except for Casperion who muttered rude things under his breath.

"Knight," the eldest dragon breathed. The others repeated it, some crackling with fire, others with electricity. Storm clouds started to gather overhead. This was, as one might expect, bad.

"Perhaps we should—" I started.

"You *dare* trespass here, Knight?" the elder dragon hissed, baring her teeth and digging her claws into the ground. All around her, loose stones began to rattle. "You *dare* threaten us?"

"Threaten *you*?" Mother scoffed. "After I have done *nothing* to you? I, who returned your eggs to you when they were stolen? I, who have kept out of your way until you started trying to *kill* me?"

"You are the last Knight. How could we stand

such a threat to exist?" a youngish-looking purple dragon asked, a sneer clear on his face.

"For generations, the Knights existed, and because I am the last, you decide, suddenly, that I deserve to die? Even though I haven't done anything to you?" Mother was furious, her tone icy and cold. It sent a chill up my spine, and I wasn't even the target of her ire. I'd never seen her so furious, not even when Baz broke her front bay window with a slingshot and blamed it on me.

"Your very existence is a threat," the young dragon snapped. "And you have done something to us. You've trespassed on our sacred lands!"

"Sacred?" I whispered, turning to Casperion. He ignored me.

"Only after you tried to kill my son and nephew for the simple crime of coming to visit me for dinner!" She was yelling, now, a sound which I had heard only once before, when she pulled me into her flat before I could be struck by lightning. "The crime is yours. I am merely here to demand justice."

"Maybe Baz should have come on this trip," Neja murmured to me. I silently agreed. He was better equipped to deal with this particular situation. Somehow, I doubted that my mother facing down two dozen angry dragons was going to do more than die in spectacular fashion.

"Justice?" the elder dragon roared. "For every one

of your kind to exist, one of us has died. More, for some of your more prolific killers! Should we forget all of this?"

"You would pin the crimes of people long past on me?" Mother was incredulous. "How is that fair?"

The elder dragon sneered. She raised a claw. "Life's not fair."

The dragons moved to strike. My mother raised her sword. Neja reached for her knives. I let the shadows inside me erupt.

My vision snapped into greyscale, yellow and gold lights illuminating the lifeforces of those around me. The dragons were threaded mostly with a silver so bright that it was impossible to ignore their immortality. They were also, however, bound with gold, a sign they could be killed. Compared to Mother and Neja, though, they were indestructible.

Along with my vision, my full Reaper form took shape. It was a mass of eldritch coils, twisting and twining around one another. My maw was full of teeth that could tear through the very fabric of existence, and my claws could rend souls. I tried to avoid emerging into this form often, as it usually resulted in the abject terror of all those who saw it. As such, I hadn't emerged fully into this form since taking Death's heart into my own, since losing the last of my humanity. Since becoming Death's heir.

Now, there was something different. Something

more. I stretched and felt enormous wings at my back. When I turned to look, they glistened with the light of the void, the space between stars. They held the end of all things within them and pulled on the world around me. I closed my eyes, calling to that pull and quieting it. Letting it settle.

When I opened my eyes again, I twisted to face the dragons. They stood before me, still as a rabbit before a wolf. I let out a snarl that rattled the sky.

"You dare to attack my family without provocation?" I asked, bringing my head closer to the elder dragon. "You dare to defy what is just and right? Are you so afraid of one human?"

"You would have us ignore our natural enemy, Great One?" the elder dragon hissed, spreading her wings. I spread out my coils, encircling the dragons. They stepped back, brushing against one another.

"If your enemy came here with an army? No. If they came here with intent to kill, to harm? No. But when you attack with no provocation, then the only conclusion that I can reach is that you, the shapers of worlds, are afraid." I pressed my coils tighter against the dragons, put my head next to the elder dragon's maw. "Are you afraid?" I whispered.

She snapped at me, teeth meeting shadow and passing right through.

I pulled back and spoke loudly enough for all to hear. "We did not come to usurp you. To invade your lands. To kill you. The Knight came to call for a cease to your attacks on her and hers. I came to find the Fisher King. That is all. Will you let us pass, or will you insist on being unreasonable? That is so unlike the dragons of whom I have heard stories."

Instead, the elder dragon began to laugh, a cruel, terrible sound. "You have not been taught much, oh Heir to Death. These lands were carved from Else-where a thousand generations ago. They were granted to us in sovereignty by Death and Life both. We rule here absolutely. And as such, we deal with those who trespass as we see fit. For you? Well, we could not harm you if we tried, and you bear the protection of Death. But the Knight? The djinn? They may have accompanied you, but they bear no such protection. They are *ours* to do with as we see fit."

Well, crap.

I hissed, wrapping my coils protectively around Mother and Neja. I had brought them here; I would see them safe.

"She is right, Deathling," Casperion said in a low voice. I rounded on him and saw a glint of some-thing in his eye for a moment before it vanished. Self-satisfaction, perhaps? Certainly, it was not fear.

"You knew this?" I asked, drawing close to the smaller dragon. He pulled his head back as I called my shadows closer, focusing on him in my fury. "You knew this and you did not tell me?"

Casperion curled a lip, revealing one fang. As if he could ever be a threat to me. He had known.

I shifted, my claws reaching for him. He danced backwards, weak wings flaring in alarm. "You knew. You thought to curry favour with the dragons who exiled you. You thought to buy back your, what, position? Life? Your friends, who have long since forgotten you, with the blood of my family?"

"She is the last Knight," Casperion growled, glaring at my mother who stood close to me, sword drawn. Neja was at her side, weapons in each hand. They both looked more afraid than I'd ever seen them. "And I delivered her here."

Mother visibly shoved her fear aside and replaced it with temper. She did not like being backed into situations. She never had. I couldn't count the number of times she'd pushed back on council rulings in the neighbourhood, or to a school board, or just at her job. She was not one to be cowed. Perhaps it was the Knight blood running through her veins, or perhaps it was just who she was. Either way, she lunged for Casperion with her sword, ready to deliver a killing blow.

She would have succeeded, too, had I not gotten in her way.

"Cal. Move!" she demanded.

"I cannot," I hissed. I turned, my sinuous form twisting and writhing. "I bargained with this worm. To bring him with us as we crossed the border of the dragon lands. To stand between him and you."

"In exchange for what?" my mother asked, incredulous. "What could possibly be worth that?"

"A guide to the Fisher King."

The elder dragon laughed, the sound like a bell just out of tune. "You would have needed no *guide* to the Fisher King, Heir to Death. Its stench spreads from the lake where it lives. Any one of us could have pointed it out to you. Instead, you took the word of a traitor. One who would never be allowed back, no matter how many Knights he delivered to our feet."

Casperion snarled wordlessly at the elder dragon. I didn't know what crime he had committed, what terrible thing he had done to earn the ire of the other dragons, but I didn't really care. He had committed a crime against me and mine, leading us into a trap.

The really terrible thing was that I should have known better.

I'd been dealing with creatures in Elsewhere long enough that I knew to never take them at their word. The Fae in particular had taught me that you should never, ever take someone at face value. I'd had more than enough experience with them, and with others, to make the lesson stick. And just once, I'd forgotten it. Eager to have assistance in a place that was anathema to my mother. I'd wanted as much help as I could get for her, to help her stop these unwarranted attacks by dragons.

Instead, I'd led her straight into a trap.

CHAPTER 9

My fury was a tangible thing, rising up through my throat like fire. My void-shaped coils became more solid, my shadows more numerous. When again I turned to Casperion, I could *feel* the edges of things, all things, at my fingertips. He sucked in a breath, smoke curling at his nostrils. Then, he took a single step back.

Afraid.

Finally.

I leaned in close, my nose nearly touching his. "My mother may not be able to harm you," I cooed in a gentle, mocking voice, "but your bargain did not stretch to me."

Casperion tried to blast me with fire, but it fizzled out before escaping his mouth. He coughed, alarmed. His fire had likely never failed him before, but then again, I doubted he'd ever been confronted with someone like me, before.

"You have lied to and betrayed me. You have bargained with me in bad faith. Therefore, I release you from your obligation to guide me to the Fisher King." The weight of the bargain on my shoulders vanished. Casperion shivered as his half of the bargain vanished.

I pulled back, curling my lip. "Unfortunately, I cannot simply kill you. You have not directly harmed me or mine. Had you done so, this would have been over the moment you betrayed us. So instead, I will give you a choice. You may fight the Lady Knight, to answer your challenge. Or you may run."

"Run?" Casperion snorted.

"Run," I whispered. "Run far away and never return. Never see the dragon lands again. Run away and know that if you try and see this place again, try to talk with anyone you knew again, that you will be pursued. I will personally hunt you down and leave your entrails for the creatures of the earth to feast upon. Your bones will be the beams of a house for goblins, your horns a trophy above my fire."

The dragon glared at me, those centuries of built-up malice burning through his eyes. He curled his claws, digging into the lush earth. For an instant, he flicked his gaze to Mother, standing calmly, sword resting point-first in the ground. He turned to the other dragons, who watched with visible interest. We both knew they would not interfere on his behalf.

He hesitated. Indecision warred with wrath in his expression. Then, finally, with a last snarl in my direction, he turned tail and fled.

My shadows retreated to me. My coils shrank. I returned to my human shape, weary in bone and thought. Mother flashed me a nod of approval. Neja rushed to my side. "Are you alright?" she asked quietly.

"Fine." I adjusted my glasses. "Fine."

"A Reaper as well as Heir to Death," the elder dragon said, obviously interested. "What a combination. The universe shifts where you step, Heir to Death. Be careful of that power, for it could be the undoing of the world as we know it."

I said nothing to her. There was nothing to say. Not to them, watching gleefully at the tableau before them. Instead, I turned to my mother, to Neja. "They are...I'm sorry."

Neja smiled sadly, squeezing my arm. "It's alright, Cal. It was my choice to come, and I'll face the consequences."

"The consequences of what? Why are you sorry?" Mother asked, looking more stern than concerned. She frowned at me until I answered.

"The dragons do have sovereignty here. And

though Casperion was a dragon and let us through the barrier, he did not have the authority to do so under the conditions of his exile. As such, we are trespassers. They dragons have stated they have no wish to interfere with me, given my position and the fact that anything they do would be…meaningless to me. But you…"

My mother's expression turned cold. Distant. "We have no such protections and are at their mercy."

Given that my mother had met Mercy, in all her terrifying glory, she knew exactly what that meant. I bowed my head in acknowledgement. Had I any vestiges of humanity left, I might have fidgeted. I might have felt an ache in my chest or a tightness in my throat. I might have rallied against the dragons and tried to fight my way out, consequences be damned. I wasn't human anymore, though. I was bound by certain rules and I knew it. So I had no choice but to stand aside.

In that moment, I missed my humanity. A great deal.

I turned to the dragons. "Would you reconsider?"

The elder dragon smiled, teeth showing. "What would you give us for such a thing?"

"What would you want?"

Neja stepped in front of me. "Cal, no! Do not make any bargains with them. Not for me."

If not for her, then who? I locked eyes with the elder dragon. She blinked slowly, knowing that she had me in check. I could move forwards without being held back, but it would mean leaving Neja and my mother behind. Leaving those I loved behind.

I might have been about to inherit Death's power and position, but I don't think even he would fault me for not wanting to sever those connections.

Everything dies, he would have said, and then stood aside to let me do what needed to be done.

"Immortality," the dragon said at last. "We want immortality. *True* immortality, as you hold. As Life holds. We can still die, as *her* kind have proven over and over. We don't want to lose any more of our own. Never again."

It could be done. I had seen the few strands of gold that flower through them when looking with my Reaper's vision. If I plucked those out, they would be entirely silver. Deathless. I'd never done such a thing personally, but instinct told me it was possible. I didn't know what the consequences would be of such an action, but I could do it.

I wouldn't, though.

"Everything dies," I told the dragon. "You would have me violate the natural order so that you can avoid the pain of loss?"

"Your refusal to do so means that *you* will feel the pain of loss. Tessana, take the Knight and the djinn. We will hold them in the cells and see if the Heir to Death reconsiders when they are beyond his grasp."

The massive dragon who had pulled the roof of the tavern reached out and snatched Neja and Mother from the ground in a blink. Mother never even had time to react, though Neja managed to stab Tessana in the toe with a dagger. The massive dragon just hissed and shook it off, like a mosquito bite.

"Cal!" Neja called as Tessana reared back, wings flaring. "Don't you dare come after us. We'll get this sorted out!"

My mother said nothing, instead fixing me in a stare that—even without any humanity remaining to me—chilled me to the bone. It was the same stare that she had given Baz's mother when she disowned her son. It was the same stare that she had given the other Thorpes in our family when she turned her back on them. It was the same stare, full of fury and ice that had sent my father packing when I was just a toddler.

This time, it was directed at me.

I held her gaze until Tessana leaped into the air and flew off, a quickly diminishing dot in the sky.

"We won't kill them," the elder dragon assured me, voice soft. "Not yet. Go to the Fisher King. Finish whatever business you have with the creature, and when you return—if you return—then we will discuss again our price for those you love."

I nodded. A simple movement, brusque, using only a few muscles. It felt like I had stones around my neck. The words slipped out before I could stop them. "Know this, Great Lady. If they come to harm under your care, then you will have forever made an enemy of me. I will see to it that you have your immortality, and I will be sure that you never die. You will live, flayed open to the sky, vultures plucking out your liver like Prometheus, forever."

"Have you the authority for such a thing?" she cooed, grinning.

"There is a regime change coming, Great Lady. As you said, the universe changes based on where I step. If I were you, I would take care not to stand in my path."

I turned away from the dragons and started walking towards the horizon. I had no idea if I was heading the right way, and my sense of direction was generally really poor, but it was the opposite direction in which I'd entered the dragon lands, so I figured it was a good start.

At the very least, I managed to work off some of my anger before I decided that I was irreparably lost.

The sun had started to set, and while the scenery remained the lovely Italian countryside, there was no stench, as the elder dragon had said, nor any other indication that I was getting any closer to, well, anything.

I found a grove of trees, dropped my rucksack, and realised that I had absolutely no idea how to start a proper fire. In all my adventures, I had always had someone with me, and those occasions which required camping out usually had me collecting the firewood and the other person starting the fire. Certainly, I could make a guess of putting the logs together, stuffing kindling underneath, but as far as actually getting a spark to start the fire, I was baffled.

I should have packed a lighter.

I was starting to think that I would have to actually twirl a twig against another piece of wood when a small voice piped up out of the twilight.

"I can help you, if you like."

"You mean *we* can help."

I don't know what I expected, but three tiny dragons tumbling out of the grasses wasn't it. Then again, this was still the dragon lands, after all. They were about the size of my forearm, with stunted wings and tiny nubs of horns on their heads. The one in the middle was slightly larger than the others, a solid black with golden eyes. The one to his left was bright, cerulean blue, her eyes a vivid orange. The third was a dull gold, her eyes pale and milky. I realised a moment later that she was blind, her tail resting on the back of the black dragon to guide her way.

"See? I can light the fire!" the cerulean female chirped, rearing her head back and blowing out her cheeks. She squeezed her eyes shut in concentration then blew violently outwards. Nothing happened.

"Ha! I knew it!" the male crowed. "You can't even produce a spark!"

"Yeah, well I'd like to see you try," the blue dragon grumbled. "Vivana says you can only blow hot air."

I was about to express my confusion when the tiny gold dragon inched her way forwards, nostrils flaring. Without acknowledging the other two, she sniffed my pile of woods then coughed onto it. Sparks flew and caught the dried grasses, catching the kindling. Within a minute, the fire had started to catch properly and was crackling away.

"Show off," the black dragon muttered, though he butted the gold dragon's head affectionately.

"I do appreciate the help," I said at last, "but who are you and what in the many realms are you doing here?"

"I'm Setar," the black said, puffing his chest out. "That's Hester, who lit your fire, and my little sister, Caris."

"A pleasure," I said drily. "I'm Cal. You didn't fully answer my question. What are you doing here? I don't imagine your parents are particularly keen about you wandering around after dark."

Setar scoffed. Caris chirped up, "These are the dragon lands! We're dragons, dummy. We can do whatever we like."

Hester sniffed me. "You don't smell like a dragon."

"That's because I'm not."

All three dragons sucked in excited gasps. They broke out into questions almost immediately, talking over one another and scrambling forward to crawl around and over me. I had some experience with small things with claws trying to climb me, given that I owned a miniature griffin ghost, but three dragons was something else.

"Enough!" I said, practically shaking them off. "Enough."

They gathered before me, staring at me with wide, eager eyes.

"You should go back to your families. They might be worried about you since I'm wandering around."

"Why, are you going to hurt us?" Setar asked. He looked baffled by the prospect. I sighed.

"No. I have no intention of hurting you."

"Then we're fine!" Hester insisted. "Why are you here, anyways? Are you going somewhere? Are you going to meet with the adults?"

"I've already met with them. And yes, I am going

somewhere." Somehow, I got the impression that these three really didn't get the concept of personal space, or privacy. I hadn't had much contact with kids in my life, but this was exactly what I had expected. Trouble.

"Fun!" Caris cried. "We'll go with you!"

"No." I shook my head. "Absolutely not."

I wasn't about to take on three new charges after just having lost my girlfriend and my mother to the adult dragons. I was still angry, for one thing. I also had no idea how to care for baby dragons.

"Pleeeeeaaaassssseee!" they begged simultaneously. I closed my eyes, pinched the bridge of my nose, and sighed.

CHAPTER 10

My thoughts were in complete disarray the next day. I'd gone from having my mother and Neja essentially kidnapped before my very eyes—with nothing I could do about it—to toting around three baby dragons as I headed to the Fisher King. The emotional whiplash was enough to make my head hurt. The constant chatter took me the rest of the way into a serious headache.

My arguments with the tiny dragons as to why they couldn't come with me had been futile. I'd tried arguing the danger of my destination, to which they'd responded that this was the dragon lands and there wasn't anything dangerous to a dragon. I'd countered *this* argument with a suggestion that their parents didn't tell them everything, which received a resounding bout of laughter. From there, I tried bribing them, scolding them, even flat out ignoring them. Short of donning my Reaper form of shadows and claws and fangs, I doubted very much that I could get rid of them.

Hester currently rode on my right shoulder as I walked, her nose lifted to the air to take in any scent that came her way. Caris and Setar alternated between running about around my feet and riding on my free shoulder or head. After a while, I gave in to the inevitable and tried to enjoy the company. I would find some way to send them on their way before we made it to the Fisher King.

"You're from the outside world, right Cal?" Setar asked, leaning over my head and peering down at my face. I brushed him back and adjusted my glasses.

"A fact we have established well," I said drily.

"So you've *seen* the outside world. What's it like? I mean, I heard there are all sorts of evil creatures out there! That everyone fights all the time and it's a constant war between creatures for food and territory and—"

"Hardly." I interrupted before his descriptions could get any more involved. "Certainly there are those who would attack any who invaded their territory, but I imagine your parents would do the same to those who tried to invade the dragon lands."

In fact, I knew they would.

"I guess," Caris said, galloping along at my feet, nose scrunched.

"Mostly, the rest of Elsewhere is a peaceful place. Beautiful, with hundreds of different landscapes and dwellings and people. The Faerie lands, for instance, are lush with life suited to the four seasonal courts. And the rock trolls live in mountains that are so tall you couldn't climb them if you tried. I live in the Lands of Silence, where Death resides, and it's right next to Life's territory, which is loud and raucous and vibrant."

I had thought myself fond of my London home, back when I was a human. I'd prided myself on a flat with a view of the city, a commute that took me through the nicer parts of London, and no desire to be anywhere else. Now I'd seen not only most of the mortal realms, but Elsewhere, too. And I found, oddly, that I loved it.

"So...the outsiders *aren't* evil?" Hester asked dubiously. Caris looked up at me eagerly then tripped over a root. I lifted her to my left shoulder and kept walking.

"No one that I've met is inherently evil. Some people are selfish. Some can be cruel when faced with those different from them, but very few have evil in them. They just look out for what's best for them, and no one else."

Setar snorted. "That's boring! I thought the outside world was supposed to be exciting."

"It's more exciting than here, I bet," Caris offered. Hester nodded.

Oh, great. Now I'd done it. The dragons would absolutely skin me alive if I instilled a sense of exploration in their young. I decided to change the subject.

"When do your wings get big enough for you to fly?" I asked. Setar started flapping his under-developed wings, jostling my head. Caris huffed.

"My mother says that my wings will grow in about five years," Hester said proudly. Then, she deflated. "She also says I shouldn't worry about it, because flying blind is dangerous."

"You can walk, can't you?" I asked. Hester nodded. "Even without assistance?"

"My nose tells me where to go," she said.

"Then why can't you fly? Does your nose stop working when you're in the air?" I was tired of being told I couldn't do something. I'd heard so many excuses. Because I was human. Because I had no soul. Because I wasn't allowed. My heart beat loudly in my chest. I had let Neja and Mother go, be taken from me, without a fight. Why? Because I was told I wasn't allowed to fight for them. For what was *mine*.

"My nose keeps working," Hester said tentatively. "Does that mean I can fly?"

"Provided your wings grow large enough, why not?" I wouldn't let anyone tell her she couldn't do something, either. The world was difficult enough without others dictating ability.

"Caris! Setar! He says I can fly!" Hester shouted, flapping her own small wings.

That tidbit of news occupied my hangers-on for the rest of the morning. When I stopped for lunch, they chased each other around in circles, flapping their wings and chattering excitedly about all the things they would see when they were old enough to fly. I rubbed my chest, pained.

When would they lose that youthful naïveté? I sincerely hoped that it wouldn't hurt, as it so often did.

A couple of hours after lunch, with the three dragons sleeping in my rucksack, I started to smell something. It was faint, barely a trace on the wind, but it was definitely there. The farther I walked, the stronger the smell got until it was almost overpowering. Rot. Rotted flesh and dead leaves in moisture. Wood that was falling apart. Decay, stagnation. The aftereffects of death, as it were.

"That smells bad," Setar said, climbing onto my shoulder and peering ahead. "What is it?"

"Something that's just as bad as it smells," I said. "Maybe you three should go back to your families, now. What's ahead, well, it's for me to deal with, not you."

Caris huffed, tossing her head clear of the rucksack. "That's not fair. We came all this way, and we're going to see it through! And besides, our parents won't care where we went. We've been gone for days before and no one minded."

"That was before I came," I pointed out. "Someone from the outside."

None of my arguments had worked before, but maybe now, with that stench in their noses, they would leave. Or, they could do exactly what they wanted without hesitation.

Hester raised her head and took a deep breath, coughing. "That's really bad," she said, burying her nose back in my rucksack. "Maybe Cal's right, Caris. I don't like that smell. Not at all."

The cerulean dragon frowned, considering her friend. She exchanged a glance with Setar, whose wings fluttered anxiously on his back. "I do kind of want to go home," she said slowly.

"Yeah," Setar agreed reluctantly. He hopped down from my shoulder, landing like a cat. "I think we had enough of an adventure. Let's go home. Come on, Hester, the ground's clear for you to jump."

Before the golden dragon could leap to the ground, a whispering hiss of a voice filled the air. "Who wanders to my domain? Young, vibrant. Full of the potential of life. Are you to free me from my curse?" It laughed, the sound somehow slimy. Setar let out a hiss, his back arching.

"Get back in my bag," I ordered the young dragon, reaching down to grab him. He leaped for my hand, but before I could catch him, something snatched him from the air.

The pleasant landscape that we'd travelled vanished, revealing a stinking lake's edge, still, brown water stinking on the shore where the husks of dead water plants lay rotting. Feet in the water stood the creature who had grabbed Setar. He was vaguely human, with the shape and dress of someone belonging to medieval times. Small but strong, a woad-blue tunic and buckskin hose, a belt of gold and a crown of the same style on his head. That was where the familiar ended. The creature's skin was leathery and worn, a mummification of human flesh such as the man they'd pulled from a bog in the mortal realms some time back. He had a beard, but it looked more like algae than hair. His face was sunken, misshapen, half-skull and half-flesh, covered with that same mummified skin. From his thigh, a reddish brown liquid dripped steadily into the lake, the only noise in this dead place.

Setar squirmed in his grasp, letting out pitiful cries and trying to claw at the creature's skin. "Let me go! Let me go!"

"No," the creature said, drawing a bony finger down the young dragon's spine. "It's been so long since I've tasted the potential that young life brings. Are you pure enough to break my curse? Are you?"

"Setar!" Caris cried out. The little black dragon struggled more fervently. Hester whimpered, burying her face in the bag. I zipped the bag shut and settled it on my shoulders, the only way I knew to keep the two young dragons safe.

"Release the child," I demanded.

The creature flicked empty eyes to me and smiled widely. "Who are you? You do not smell like you should."

I wondered briefly what I smelled like and decided I would rather not know. Instead, I said again, "Release the child."

The creature sniffed Setar like I would a freshly baked pie. The young dragon whimpered, looking at me with wide eyes. "I think…not."

My eyes still locked with Setar's, the creature opened his mouth and devoured the young dragon in one bite. Had Caris and Hester been watching, they would have screamed. As it was, I nearly did so myself before remembering that they could still hear what was happening, even if they couldn't see it.

"You shouldn't have done that," I said, tears pricking my eyes.

"Oh? Why not?" the creature asked, smiling widely. "What are you going to do about it?"

"Me?" I asked, taking the bag off and setting it down several feet from the edge of the lake, far enough away from the creature that it would have to go through me to get to it. "I'm going to kill you."

The creature laughed. That was its last mistake.

I exploded outwards in shadow and emptiness, wrapping the half-dead monster in my coils. It let out a singular gasp before I had my claws wrapped around its throat. But where I should have seen the colour of life and energy settling around the creature like an aura, I saw nothing. I saw no gold, no yellow, no silver. Just the muddy, indistinct brown of the lake, pulsing as the creature tried to breathe through my stranglehold.

It clawed at my coils, trying to do damage, but I was beyond that sort of pain. I held the creature in the air and dug my claws into its belly, digging out where its stomach should have been. Trying to rescue Setar. I had failed the people around me enough and it was time I put an end to that. So I dug through the creature's entrails, but there was no hint of the young dragon. There was no hint of anything at all. It appeared as though this creature hadn't eaten for centuries, so desiccated were its innards.

I snarled and ripped the creature in two, a movement so easy that it was like tearing paper. I tossed the pieces aside, already drawing myself back into human shape, a desperate hollowness in the pit of my stomach. Setar was gone, and I hadn't been able to save him. I hadn't been able to save anyone. Not the dragon. Not my mother. Not Neja.

I sank to my knees next to my rucksack and wrapped my arms around it protectively. "I'll never let anyone hurt you," I promised.

"You should be careful of the bargains you make."

I whirled, putting the bag behind me. The creature stood there, same as before, as though I hadn't dug through its innards and torn it in half. For the first time in a very, very long time, I felt fear.

"What are you?" I asked.

The creature tossed its head back and laughed. "Haven't you guessed? I'm the Fisher King. It is a pleasure to meet you."

CHAPTER 11

The Fisher King. This decaying creature was the Fisher King. I was speechless in my confusion.

Somewhere between my mother's almost-romanticised descriptions of the Fisher King and the relationship to the Arthurian legends, and Casperion's description of a creature that hungered endlessly, I was expecting to see either a well-dressed man of noble mien, or a black blob that devoured everything in its path. The creature before me was rotting, certainly grotesque, but it was hardly a threatening thing. At least, not until I'd seen it swallow Setar whole.

"I see I've surprised you," the creature chuckled, sketching a bow. "Not expecting to find me?"

"I was expecting you to be slightly less pathetic," I

said, standing. I put my bag on again to better protect Hester and Caris, who were wriggling in the bag, obviously scared.

The Fisher King blinked at my words as if not expecting insults. I didn't know the legends and lore surrounding this thing, not nearly as well as my mother or Casperion seemed to, but I doubted insulting it was par for the course. "Who are you?" it asked.

"Cal Thorpe," I said.

"And why are you here, Cal Thorpe?" The Fisher King drew closer. "People don't come here without a reason. Without a purpose. Even if they all fall to me in the end."

"I'm here to see the return of the Reapers," I said. Then, because I couldn't contain it, "And to see you suffer for that dragon."

The Fisher King seemed delighted by my answer. "You're a hero, then! Come to break my curse and see to it that wrongs are righted. I do love heroes. Especially false heroes, as so many of them prove to be. They taste truly marvellous when they fall before me."

I rolled my eyes, quite visibly. My irreverence seemed to further irritate the Fisher King. He glowered at me.

"Who are you?" he asked again.

"Cal Thorpe. Like I told you."

"That tells me nothing! A name given by a Fae will provide answers. But you are no Fae, and your name holds no meaning for me." He started pacing, his steps making sucking sounds in the mud on the stagnant lake's edge. "You have power, obviously, but what sort? How far does it stretch? You tell me nothing!"

"Frankly, that's not really my problem," I said. "Now, are you going to release the Reapers? Return that dragon child?"

I knew, somehow, that Setar was still alive. I knew that I would have felt his death if he'd been snuffed out right in front of me. But even after tearing the Fisher King apart, I'd found no sign of him. If he could be found, I would find him. I vowed it, for the sake of the two dragons still hiding in my rucksack.

"Why would I do that?" He paused in his pacing to smile at me.

I took a single step closer. "Because I asked it of you. Because you keep asking me to end your curse. And because killing children—any children—is wrong."

"The dragon is not dead," the Fisher King said, rolling his eyes.

"I know. If he were, you would find yourself torn into a thousand pieces and scattered to all the corners of Elsewhere."

"Even at the cost of your Reapers?"

"Even then."

Rather than terrify him, which I had hoped, this seemed merely to delight him. The Fisher King clapped his hands together once and bowed at the waist, a mocking movement that had me wanting to strangle him again.

"You are indeed a hero! I've not had this much fun in centuries!" Suddenly all business, he straightened and lifted his chin, a parody of the authority of kings playing across his mutilated features. "Do you know who I am?"

This had the formal sound of a riddle, the sort that the Fae liked to bandy about when trying to trick mortals to their bidding. I knew how to deal with the Fae, mostly, but this was something entirely different. I ignored the desperate squeaks from inside my bag and shifted it on my shoulder, tightening the strap.

"You are the Fisher King."

He scoffed. "A nickname, only. I am the last in my line. A guardian of the cup, of the cauldron, which brings everlasting life to the world."

"The dragons say you are a hunger, set to devouring everything in your path. Given what I've seen, I would be more inclined to believe their story than yours." Anger flared in me again at the loss of

Setar. At all the loss I'd incurred on this wretched quest.

His expression darkened. "Do you know what it is to be set to guard a thing? To always keep it from any but the true, but the righteous? I was injured, bound here by my inability to ride or walk. They said it was a price for my sins, for my...indiscretions. But how much simpler it is to have a guardian who will not wander. Who will always stay."

"The dragons bound you here," I said. "Or so they say. After having destroyed most of their lands, I've been informed."

This got a reaction out of him. "*Their* lands? *My* lands! Mine! Until my injury meant I could not travel, could not maintain that which belonged to me. My weakness seeped into the land and everything rotted and died. And still I am bound here. For what? The testing of heroes?"

I'd been to a proving ground of heroes before. It was meant to test their mettle, their resourcefulness. I, of course, had cheated on my way through and angered the forgotten gods who ruled over that particular demesne. They'd died at my hand shortly later.

"Why must heroes be tested?" I asked. "Why feel the need to break those who are only trying to help?"

"How can they be heroes otherwise?"

I couldn't tell if the question was genuine or sarcastic. I answered anyways. "If that's all heroes are—people broken by impossible tasks set on their shoulders—then everyone I've ever met is a hero. Surely there must be some other measure. Some other guide."

The Fisher King frowned. I could see him thinking, considering my words. In the end, though, I saw also when he decided to stop playing word games with me, when he decided to take action. "Your words have no power here, Cal Thorpe, no matter how you might wish it. This is my domain, what little left of it I have, and I hold the power. If you wish the return of the Reapers, if you wish the return of your dragon, then you will do as I ask."

I set my jaw and said nothing. The bag on my back was squirming, squeaking, and I wished desperately that I had transformed into my Reaper self and scared all three dragons away when I'd had the chance. I wished I hadn't let them come with me at all.

"The cup is on an island in the middle of this lake. It is guarded by a force so powerful even I may not approach. Defeat this force, bring me the cup, and I will set you the next task."

"I thought you were its guardian?" I said, already trying to look across the lake. The Fisher King scowled, thunderous.

He continued speaking, his words short and

sharp and nowhere near answering my question. "The water is deadly to all who touch it. All except the pure. Should you make it to the island, the guardian there will determine your worth."

"And then what? I tap dance with an octopus for your pleasure?" Already I was kneeling to pull off my shoes. Surreptitiously, I set the bag down on the ground and unzipped it. Immediately, Caris and Hester poked their heads out, starting to peep. I wrapped my fingers around their muzzles.

"You will run, as fast and as far as you can," I murmured so only they could hear. Caris mumbled something through my fingers. "I will bring Setar back. This I swear to you."

Hester wriggled, trying to escape my grasp.

"Run!" I cried, pulling the dragons free and sending them on their way. Behind me, I heard the Fisher King hiss and snarl, his steps slow thanks to the mud.

"You have tricked me," he snarled. "Bringing more than yourself here, to this sacred place. More than those who intend to fulfil the tasks."

"And you *ate* a child," I retorted, my vision going grey and shadows dancing around me. "They are no part of this. You *will* let them go."

The Fisher King hissed wordlessly, but he seemed unable to leave the boundaries of the lake, and the young dragons had already scampered back into the pleasant Italian countryside. Safe. For now.

I took off my shoes and socks and jumper, leaving me in trousers and an undershirt. There wasn't much point in trying to salvage my clothes, since they were already ruined by the hard travel, but I hated swimming with shoes on, and jumpers were nothing but heavy when soaked through. I lay my rucksack on top of the pile and, touching the pocket where I kept my phone, thought of Neja and Mother. Cold, shivering, trapped in a dragon dungeon or worse.

No. I needed to get this done. I could sort their situation and my regrets out later. Right now, I had to find this cup for the Fisher King.

Without another word to the monster, I stepped into the lake and started swimming. I heard his laughs from the shore long after I lost sight of land.

The lake was, as he had said, toxic. I could feel the water leeching energy from my bones. My skin burned at every touch of water, which, given I was swimming, was a lot. I wasn't even going to try and pretend that I was "pure" enough to survive this lake's touch. I knew there was blood on my hands. A fair bit of it at this point. I wasn't righteous or heroic. I was Cal. Nothing more, no matter much power was at my disposal.

So I burned in that toxic lake. My body fell apart,

agony replacing coherent thoughts until it was nearly impossible to keep swimming. I lifted my hand out of the water to paddle a little farther and saw only bone. Then, I died.

I think I died twice in that lake crossing. I was not a particularly fast swimmer at the best of times, and moving through the unimaginable pain was a challenge I would much rather not repeat. But each time, my body fell apart and I pushed onwards out of sheer necessity.

Then, blistering and burned, skin hanging on by mere threads, I felt ground beneath my feet. Before I could collapse into the blissful white emptiness that was death, I saw a figure standing above me. Beautiful. Ghostly. She smiled benevolently and touched me on the brow.

The pain vanished. My thoughts twisted into confusion. I couldn't quite grasp where I was, what I was doing. There were memories of my mother, but I couldn't tell if it was something I imagined, or if they were a dream. Was she in trouble? Or was I?

Knowing me, it was likely my fault. I'd forgotten her birthday, hadn't I? Surely there was nothing that would bring about this feeling of dread quite like forgetting her birthday.

Right?

I rubbed my eyes, trying to clear them of the grit that seemed to always linger there before I'd finished my first cup of coffee. I stretched. Sighed. Tossed my phone down and watched it slide with no small satisfaction across the table until it was out of immediate reach. If someone wanted to talk with me about their latest marketing proposal, they would have to be worth me reaching for it.

The door to my office swung open and I caught a glimpse of the rest of the firm. After my promotion to Vice President of Harcourt Marketing, I'd been moved to a corner office with a spectacular view of London outside my window and a spectacular view of the office from the door.

"Your two o'clock is here, Mr. Thorpe," a chirpy young voice said. Amy Knowles, my new assistant. She'd been a week on the job and I already couldn't get on without her.

"My two o'clock?" I asked, somewhat groggy still. I needed more coffee.

"That fantasy book publishing person? With the story about the dragons and King Arthur?"

I frowned, something nagging at the back of my mind. Absently, I looked out the window, not sure why I expected to see angels and giants there, battling over London. Maybe I'd stayed up too late watching movies. I was a sucker for special effects. And popcorn.

"Of course, Amy," I said. "Show them in! And while you're at it..."

"Another cup of coffee coming right up, Mr. Thorpe," she said with a wink. I grinned and leaned back in my chair.

Oh, yes. Vice President at a top-tier marketing agency in London, the best place in the world? Why would I want to be anywhere else?

CHAPTER 12

I was sitting in an overstuffed club chair near my window, my two o'clock appointment sitting across from me. He was a strange looking fellow, tall, his features extraordinarily gaunt, his skin darker than night, with a tinge of something…else. His eyes were empty—not devoid of emotion, but actually empty sockets that nevertheless held the vastness of the universe in their depths. Certainly I could see why he was perfect for a fantasy publishing company. He fit the mould exactly.

He was also familiar. A thought tugged at the back of my mind and I tried to place where I'd seen him before.

"It's quite the view," he said, gazing out the

window. I took a sip of my coffee and nodded, not really looking.

"Indeed."

"All those souls, going about their daily lives, building monuments to their own hubris," he continued. One minute, he was sitting, the next he stood before the window, hands clasped behind his back. "I've always admired them."

"Who? Londoners?" I joined him at the window. "Well, we are a tenacious bunch, certainly. Though, we can be quite fickle if things are out of sorts. I expect that's just an English trait."

The man cast me an amused look. "You English are no more or less tenacious than others of your kind."

My...kind? I frowned, not quite sure how to respond to this. We were meant to be talking about a book publicity deal. They were a small publishing outfit and wanted to get a bigger presence for their next release. It was going to be huge, if things were done right.

Before I could ask for details on the book, he spoke again. "I've always wondered how it is that your kind can hold the knowledge of imminent endings and joy in the living in equal measure. Your lives are so brief, one would think that you should be constantly worried about dying. Instead, you create empires and music. You paint and you dance and you while away your time watching silly movies and scrolling through your social media, as if you don't have time slipping through your grasp."

"Is this to do with the book...?" I asked tentatively. Maybe he was pitching me on the theme of the story, suggesting a marketing campaign. If he was, then no wonder his firm came to me; it was a terrible campaign.

"Why do you do this?" He turned his back on the window and studied me.

"What? Marketing?" I shrugged. He gave a small smile and tilted his head. "Well, I guess I'm good at it."

I was really good at it. But I could tell that wasn't the answer he wanted, and I wasn't satisfied with it, either. I sat back in my chair and frowned.

"When I was a kid, my father left. He was some big business man, and it wasn't really a surprise for a lot of reasons. But he left behind a slew of ruined reputations in his wake. Mostly small businesses, the sort that you still see sometimes on the corner. They tried to get my mother to help them, but she couldn't. Didn't know how. I helped them instead, years later, designing advertisements, telling them how to counteract the damage that had been done. I just told them what sort of things I would like to see in a business like that, and knowing what I did about my father, I was able to fix it. I didn't much care for my father, but he left me with a problem to fix. And I fixed it. I fixed it so well that it landed me here."

There had been a lot of steps in between now and then, but it was the gist of matters that counted. A moment later I frowned. Why had I told that story? I never talked about my father. It was as if he didn't exist to me. When I talked about marketing, I talked about the thrill of seeing a client succeed, or the joy of a well-crafted campaign. Not being so good at fixing someone else's mistakes that I didn't choose my own life. Not…that.

He gave me a lingering, sad smile. "Do you regret what happened?"

What had happened? I had fixed my father's mistakes, not made things worse.

There was a sound, like a crack but more insistent, and I whirled around, looking for it. Had that been a gunshot? No, surely not.

"Look, I don't really understand what's happening," I said. "But unless you want to talk about marketing for your book, then I need to get back to work."

The man looked me over, expression calm. "Perhaps we should try a different way."

I blinked, and we were on the roof of my building. Wind whipped my hair and tugged at my suit. I shivered, yelped, and staggered back from the edge.

"What's going on?" I shouted over the wind.

"You tell me," he said, standing there with his hands in his pockets, completely unruffled by the wind. "What do you see?"

I gulped and turned my attention to the city. "It's London! Just the city."

"And these are the boundaries of your world?" He took a step closer. "Is there nothing more that you want? Is there nothing else out there that calls to you?"

I peered out over the city. If I looked closely, I could see the general vicinity of my flat. And over there was my mother's flat. And...I narrowed my eyes, adjusted my glasses. What was that mist at the edges of the city? I turned, but no matter which direction I looked, the mist was there. It was as if the world didn't exist beyond London. Beyond this corner of the world.

"I..." My words caught in my throat. "I like London," I insisted.

He nodded. "I can see that. But what of your friends? What of your family?"

"My mother lives just over there." I pointed in the general direction of her home. "But she's not there right now, because....because..."

Why wasn't she at home? I knew with absolute certainty that she wasn't there, but where was she? Not within the limits of the mist-bound city. Where, then?

"But there's my cousin Baz," I continued. "He's…"

He wasn't here, either. I knew it. Why? He loved this city. Had never wanted to be anywhere else.

The man tilted his head. "And your friends? What of them? Surely you cannot spend all your time here at the office, fixated on your past?"

I snorted. "Of course not! I spend time with…with…"

There was a blank space where a person should have been, but I knew we spent time together. Watched soap operas. Ate popcorn. I frowned. What was her name? And why had I forgotten it?

"Her name is…" I took a deep breath, searching the confines of my mind. "Yolanda!"

The man's expression brightened a fraction, a smile touching his mouth. "Good. Tell me about Yolanda."

"She's a bit ridiculous. Loves popcorn more than anything else in the world. She gets confused with colloquialisms, but can make herself understood in almost any circumstance. She'd do anything for her friends." I was smiling, now, the words flowing freely. "I…I think she's my assistant? No, Amy Knowles is my assistant. Hired on last week."

"Where does Yolanda live?" he asked, stepping a little closer to the edge of the building, unconcerned by the height or the wind.

I frowned. She lived…somewhere other than

London. Somewhere else. "Elsewhere," I murmured. Was that a place? A real place? I shook my head, pounding pressure building up at the base of my skull. "What are you doing here? If you want my help with marketing your book, then—"

"Would you give up everything you have for this life? This day-to-day dance of marketing and offices and assistants getting you coffee? Your commute from home to here and back again?"

"It's a good life," I insisted. "Why would I need to give everything up?"

"Is this truly what you want? Spending your whole life making up for the past of someone else?" he asked, not answering my question. "Don't you want wonder? Don't you want to do something worthwhile?"

"What I do *is* worthwhile," I said, but suddenly I wasn't so sure. Maybe I had been spending too long fixing what was broken by someone else. Maybe I had spent too long trying to make things right. Trying to instil order on something that I should have left alone. But what else was there? "What... what sort of wonder?"

His smile grew a little wider.

I blinked again and suddenly we were standing on the ledge of the roof, the pavement spreading below us like a distant river. I yelped and tried to back up, but he lashed out and grabbed my arm, holding me in place. Poised at the edge.

"What the hell?!" I screamed.

"What if I told you that you could jump and you wouldn't die? What if I told you that wonder beyond your wildest imagination existed beyond the edge, beyond the jump?" He beamed at me.

"You're insane!" I shouted. "I'll die!"

"Will you?"

I hesitated. The wind tugged at my suit as if trying to pull me forwards, pull me off the edge.

"Why didn't you remember Yolanda? Why can't you remember where Baz is? Where your mother is?"

I frowned. It had been a long day, that was all. I hadn't had enough coffee. I was tired. I was so tired. My eyes drooped and my body swayed. I nearly lost my balance and windmilled my arms to steady myself.

My heart pounded loudly in my ears, nearly blocking out the sound of the wind.

"Who are you?" I couldn't even remember *his* name.

"Who are you?" he parroted, fixing me in that empty gaze. I couldn't look away. There was nothing there to grab me, yet it held. Held until I could see the edges of the universe, the endings of stars, the expanse that lay beyond the beyond. I couldn't breathe.

He blinked and my lungs filled. I fell to my knees on that ledge, gripping the concrete and steel tightly, holding myself in place. He crouched in front of me, unconcerned by the height, by the narrow ledge, by any of it.

"Who are you?" he asked again.

"I'm…" I licked my lips, mouth dry. "I'm Cal Thorpe, Vice President at Harcourt Marketing."

"Are you? Tell me again. Who are you?"

"I'm Cal Thorpe! I was going to be Vice President at Harcourt Marketing." The words were my own, but the details were wrong. Was going to be? No. I was. Wasn't I?

"Again."

"I'm Cal Thorpe. I—" My mind fractured at that sharp crack. It didn't just sound like a gunshot, it *was* a gunshot. In my mind's eye, I saw a park. I saw a desperate man. I heard a dog bark. I felt my end.

I pressed a hand to my side. Blood coated my fingers.

My heart beat louder still.

"Who *are* you?" he asked, voice a whisper.

"I'm Cal Thorpe," I gasped, vision tunnelling to the blood on my hand. "I'm Cal Thorpe and…and I… I died in a park before I could become Vice President at Harcourt Marketing."

He stood, nodding. "Very good."

I looked up at his figure, imposing and impossible. No person—no *human*—could look as he did. Look as though they held the end of all things within them. My heart beat so loudly I couldn't hear much of anything. Still, I asked, "Who are *you*?"

He grinned, flashing his teeth. "Haven't you figured it out? I'm *you*. The you that embraced the wonder. The you that embraced your life and never looked back. That didn't waste time on regrets. The you that *lived*."

My breath caught. I saw the mist-bound city and knew, without doubt or fear, that this place was a choice. Perhaps the biggest choice I'd ever make. Stay in the past, fixing mistakes that weren't mine, or move forwards. There would be mistakes, surely, but there would also be something else. Something more.

"Do you regret what happened?" he asked.

Did I regret what? Dying in the park?

Wait. I hadn't died in the park. There had been a man, so similar to the one standing above me, sitting on a bench. He'd offered me a job. Who was he? I closed my eyes shut. Who was he to save me from my own demise? My own death?

My eyes flew open.

"You remember, now," he said. "Good."

"What must I do?"

"Make your choice. Do you want to go back to how things were? Do you want what you left behind? Or, even knowing what pain and loss awaits you should you continue, do you want to move forward?"

Pain and loss?

My mother. Neja. The young dragon. More. I was immortal, now, the heir to Death. I would outlive them all. I would see those I loved wither and die, and I would be there to free them from their lives. I would be there to free them all from their lives. Every living being. No matter how good or bad their ending. It would be excruciating, to lose it all.

And it would be necessary.

"Everything dies, Cal," the man before me said. He reached out a hand, helping me to my feet. Why hadn't I noticed before that we were the same height? That the suit he wore was the one I wore? That our features were the same, underneath all the weight of endings? He was me. The heart that beat in my chest. The end of all things.

"But in order to die," I said slowly, the words like rocks in my mouth, "don't they first have to have lived?"

He nodded once.

I turned to the city and the river of pavement below. "Then let them live. Let them all live."

I lifted my right foot, closed my eyes, spread my eyes, and waited for my heart to beat.

Once.

Twice.

Three times.

I curled my lips in a smile and pitched forwards. The wind roared in my ears, screaming all my regrets. The ground rushed up to meet me, inexorable and final. I died, painfully.

Then, I opened my eyes and started to live. On my terms, this time.

CHAPTER 13

I pitched forwards, a splitting headache making the world spin. I had been laying on the ground, on this island in the middle of the lake. The lake that burned all my skin off. Twice. Then, I remembered, I'd crawled to shore and met with—

I scrambled to my feet and whirled, looking for the ghost.

She frowned at me, her beautiful features marred with frustration and confusion. "You should not have woken," she said. "I felt your thoughts, felt your soul. You are no hero. Only heroes can survive the temptations that I offer."

I looked down and realised that I was wearing the suit that I'd had in my dream world. Thank goodness for that. There was nothing like confronting angry people after having all your clothes burned off. I was not at my best level of politeness while in the nude.

I straightened my tie, adjusted my glasses, and faced the ghost head on. She was beautiful, like a statue of marble from a thousand years ago. Her hair tumbled over her shoulder and swayed in a wind that existed only for her. The rest of the island, shrouded in mist and obscurity, was completely still.

"Perhaps it would be easiest to start with an introduction," I suggested. "I'm Cal Thorpe—"

She waved my words away. "Yes. I saw you in your small little world. Cal Thorpe, Vice President of Harcourt Marketing, whatever that is."

I sighed. "First of all, marketing is a means by which certain people trying to sell a product, service, or idea to a people use to achieve that goal. Whether that be word of mouth, or with advertisements in social media, or on videos, or even by having celebrities endorse their products."

The ghost blinked, looking taken aback. "What?"

"Secondly, I'm *not* the Vice President at Harcourt Marketing. That's rather the point, isn't it?"

"I don't think—"

"Now, I will freely admit that I am not a hero. I haven't got the time or the inclination for such a thing. I am here only to retrieve the cup, go *back* across that stupid lake, and free the Reapers—and anyone else that the Fisher King has devoured. So. Where is it?"

The ghostly woman huffed. "Where is what?"

"This cup that I'm meant to fetch."

She waved her arms. "Look around! Go ahead. I'll wait."

I seemed to be ruining everyone's day by not being the hero they wanted. Well, tough. I lifted my chin and started walking. The mist parted for me, swirling around my ankles like an over-eager puppy. The lake hadn't been massive, so I wasn't surprised when my circuit of the island only took a few minutes. I saw grass, some mossy boulders, the skeleton remains of a small tree, even a few stones that looked as though they'd been hewn at some point. Ruins? If so, they were almost completely devoured.

No matter how I looked, though, there was no cup. No cauldron. Not even a rock that looked like it might hold a mouthful of water in its curves.

I returned to the beach where the ghost waited. "So. No cup?"

She shook her head. "No cup."

"Then why did the Fisher King send me here?"

The ghost adjusted the folds of her dress and

tilted her head. Had she been alive, I would say she was trying to get the light to shine on her in a more appealing manner. As a ghost, though, it just shone through her. "This place is a proving ground for heroes."

Another one? Great.

"I've been to one of those before. It was basically defunct, run by a bunch of old, forgotten gods. I'm assuming that this is different?"

She sniffed. "This place has naught to do with gods, remembered or forgotten. This is a place for introspection. For the proving of righteousness. For the testing of a hero's heart. You have passed my test, though I don't know how, which means you must move on to the next stage."

"To find the cup, right? Because—"

"Yes, yes, the Fisher King demands it." The ghost looked annoyed. I wondered how long she'd been trapped here, messing with people's hopes and dreams to try and weed out those she considered worthy. Heroism was so subjective; I was amazed that any heroes ever managed to exist.

"Look," I said. "I think we may have gotten off on the wrong foot. I'm just trying to get through this… quest. I need to get the cup back to the Fisher King so I can rescue the Reapers. It's nothing personal, my not wanting to linger. And really, I don't even take offence at the whole messing with my brain thing. I get it. But if you could be a little more succinct with your explanations and instructions, I would be grateful."

The ghost looked like she was about to cry.

"For centuries, I have visited the dreams of heroes and those who would claim to be heroes. I have seen their hopes and their goals and I have seen them view temptation and fail. And never once have they turned to me and asked how to break *my* curse. Only they search for the cup. Search for what will cure the Fisher King."

Stars and stones. Was she *jealous*?

I pinched the bridge of my nose, closing my eyes. "I get that this is probably not your ideal job, but you can't blame me for it."

"And still you do not ask what can be done for me!"

I'd just about had enough. I had, in the last few days, trekked across Elsewhere on the back of an ostrich. I had been led by a lying dragon into a land of creatures that very much wanted to cause me harm, but couldn't, because I was, well, me. Instead, they kidnapped my mother and my girlfriend, and I had let it happen because I was beholden by some legal loophole, having basically trespassed. I'd befriended three dragon children, lost one of them to a complete ass of a creature, and had my skin sloughed off by an acidic lake. I had decided, definitively, that I wanted this life, pain and all, but deciding it and dealing with reality were two very different things. I was very much *not* in the mood to deal with a ghost with self-worth issues.

"What would you have me do?" I asked with a hiss. I let a little of my Reaper powers bleed forward, the world going from colour to grey. I could see the strands of energy surrounding the ghost. It wasn't like seeing the auras of the living, in their shades of yellow or immortal silver. This was like most of the energy had been bled away, leaving only strands holding her together. A weaving, with most of the weft pulled away.

The ghost sucked in a breath at my new gaze. She retreated. I stepped forwards.

"Would you have me finish unravelling your life? Would you have me kill you—again? I can do that. Your curse would end, as surely as the sun rises." I took another step towards her. She shrank into herself.

"Maybe…maybe if you just—"

"If I just…? What? As you said before, my lady, I'm no hero. I am not going to swear myself to your cause, only to face another being down the line who demands their curse broken. And another after that. I haven't got the time to play these games. The

Fisher King has something I want, and I intend to get it back. Do you understand?"

To my surprise, she bowed to me. "Yes. I understand. Death has come for me at last."

Silvery ghost tears fell from her eyes, landing on the ground and making the mist swirl. Great, now I'd made her cry.

"I have waited so long for this day. For so long did I think that maybe I would find a hero who could traverse the questing and set me free. But if I am released from my burdens, what care have I as to the method. No, it will be better this way. To rest."

I really hated quests. "Fine. Don't get all noble and self-sacrificing on me, now. What do I have to do to find this cup and break your curse and break the Fisher King's curse? Is there another island? Another lake?"

She fixed me in her gaze with a frown. "I don't understand. Is this not what you—"

"Just. Tell. Me," I growled. "Before I change my mind."

"You must travel the stair into the depths. There, you will meet with a being who will test your strength of body, as I have tested your strength of mind. At the centre of this beast's lair is a door. Go through this door and you will face the last of us. He who holds the cup, and the sword, and the key to our freedom."

Sword? What sword? I was about to ask when the mist vanished. Where the ruins had been, the ground shifted and churned, revealing a stairway that led straight into the earth. The ghostly woman was gone.

"I really, really hate quests," I snarled to no one. Death and I were going to have a long conversation when I returned. One about my job requirements and future quests.

I went to the stair and started climbing down.

And down.

And down.

And down.

After the light from the surface had vanished and I had lost count of the stairs, I sat on the edge of one of the steps. My calves burned. I was wheezing. I wish I'd thought to ask for some water or something before I set out on this particular journey. Actually, a cup of coffee would have been great right about then.

I peered into the darkness and wondered how many more steps I had to descend. Then, I wondered if it would be simpler just to fall and risk breaking my neck on the way. I would recover, and while it would hurt, it wouldn't be nearly as annoying as climbing a thousand or more steps.

No, I didn't like pain enough to do that.

With a sigh, I stood and continued down the

stairs. After a while, my eyes adjusted fully to the darkness and I was able to see a few of the details. The stairs were carved straight from rock and were worn with the passage of time. The walls were reasonably smooth, broken only occasionally by a spot where a rock had been chipped away. I half-expected carvings of great battles and heroes, but instead, there was nothing.

I wondered if the point of this particular challenge was to die of boredom.

Finally, after approximately an eternity, I stumbled when my foot met flat ground instead of another stair. I windmilled my arms and smacked into the wall.

"Are you well?" a voice asked. It was the sort of voice you would encounter after a particularly embarrassing fall in the middle of a crowded tube station: unfailingly polite, infinitely more refined than you, and evidence that your fall had been witnessed. For me, it was also proof that I wasn't alone in this, well, whatever it was. Underground dungeon. Torture chamber. Something.

"I'll survive," I said, the only possible response to such a question. I straightened, brushed off my suit jacket, and turned to face my witness.

Had I any remaining sense, I would have screamed, turned tail, and climbed those stairs again. Unfortunately for the monster standing before me, I had no sense remaining at all. It was impossibly large for such a small corridor, massive shoulders brushing against the walls on either side, head hunched to keep from hitting the ceiling. Horns that could impale me with ease curved forwards from the monster's forehead, scraping off rocks from the ceiling with every movement. It was furry, slightly, and had a head that looked more bovine than human, with a body that looked like it belonged to the biggest of Scotland's caber tossers.

A minotaur.

"Huh," I said, frowning.

"Huh? Not the usual sort of reaction," he said, looking concerned. "Are you sure you didn't hit your head on the way down?"

"Quite certain, though I can't make any promises for my early childhood." I adjusted my glasses, squinted in the dim light—where were the lights coming from, anyways—and said, "Huh," again.

"What is it?" the minotaur asked, twisting his head and scraping the ceiling, as if looking for something.

"Well, it's just, I thought your kind were more associated with Greek mythology than Arthurian legends, which is where I seem to be stuck."

He blinked. "Oh. Well. You see, it's not as if I *chose* this particular line of work, after all. It's a—"

"Let me guess. A curse?"

The minotaur nodded. "Indeed. And while I'm terribly sorry about it, the parameters of my curse require me to test your strength."

"Meaning?" I had a bad feeling about this.

"I'm going to have to kill you."

CHAPTER 14

hy was it, that when I encountered a new person or creature or anything of the sort, that their first reaction was to try and kill me? Was I that terrible of a person that my evil deeds spread before me like a plague and filled everyone with a murderous rage? Was I ugly beyond repair? It just didn't seem fair.

The part of my brain still capable of logical thought realised that I was growing delirious from lack of sleep, the psychological trauma of the last few days, and the fact that I'd skipped more than one meal recently. I was tired, hungry, and pissed off, in essence.

I didn't, as such, take the minotaur's threat, no matter how polite, very well.

I pulled my Reaper abilities forwards, letting my

vision melt away into grey and white and black. My skin became shadowed, my heartbeat slowed. I wasn't the eldritch horror of scales and coils and claws that was the full manifestation of my abilities, but the minotaur cowered anyways.

"You dare to threaten me?" I asked in a low voice.

"I only seek to test your strength!" the minotaur said, hunching his shoulders even more. His bull's tail whipped behind him in agitation. "It's part of my curse!"

I smiled coldly. "Ah, yes, this curse. A curse upon you. A curse upon the ghost at the island. A curse upon the Fisher King. How many more curses are there for me to break? Perhaps I should ask instead who cursed you and go straight to the source. Kill *them*."

The minotaur whimpered. "Please. It's my duty, that's all."

I huffed. "Yes, yes, your duty."

I fixed my gaze on the minotaur, seeking his aura. Unlike the emptiness of the Fisher King, or the thready nature of the ghost, the minotaur's lifeforce was perfectly normal. Oh, he had the faint pulse of silver immortality, but otherwise he glowed a perfect marigold yellow. Bright and vibrant and lively.

I reached out and brushed my fingers over his aura. He flinched and shivered.

"Truly," I asked, my words barely audible. "Do you wish to test my strength, even now?"

He shivered again. "Milord, I must."

I gestured, my hand sweeping the air. "Then lead the way."

I followed the minotaur, hunched and afraid, through the cavern. Occasionally, the ceiling and walls opened up a bit to reveal nooks and cracks, but mostly it was small and cramped. I lost track of the twists and turns that we took to make it through the cavern, but it wasn't a labyrinth, as there were no diversions, only a straight line.

Eventually, the walls fell away and the ceiling rose enough that the minotaur could stand tall without scraping his horns. The room was not massive, but big enough to move freely in. Big enough for a battle.

On the far side of the room, on a shelf carved into the wall, was a simple goblet made of some corroded metal. Beside the cup was a sword, gleaming and silver, hanging from a stand on the wall. The objects I was meant to retrieve, I presumed.

The minotaur didn't seem to notice my scrutiny of the objects. He only waved a hand to a pile of rubbish in a corner. "You may pick a weapon, if you like."

Indeed, the pile was formed of weapons of all

sorts. Axes, shields, staffs, spears, swords, knifes, more. Any conceivable weapon was there, all piled together as if carelessly thrown. I looked closer and saw that many were speckled with rust, as if they'd never been cleaned after drawing blood. And beneath a few of the handles were what looked like bones.

It wasn't a pile of weapons, I realised as I spotted more bone throughout the handles and shields. It was a pile of the dead.

"How long have you been here?" I asked. The minotaur shrugged.

"I sleep for a time between heroes," he said. "I am not aware of the passage of time when I sleep. But… it has been many, many years."

I felt a rustle of pity in my chest. Not just for him, but for the ghost, who was able only to dream by manipulating the dreams of others. The Fisher King could rot for all I cared. The other two, though, felt more like victims to me than willing participants.

"Which weapon will you use?" the minotaur asked, squaring up to me with a reluctant look.

"No weapons." I was a terrible fighter. My soul had learned how to defend himself while on the run for five hundred years, but I, personally, had always been really bad at fighting. Even after reuniting with my soul, my abilities with weapons and defence were pathetic. I was better suited to chess matches or board room discussions over coffee. Or tearing people limb from limb with my Reaper shadows.

Subtlety in combat was not my style.

"No weapons? But I could kill—" The minotaur paused, looking me over. "You do not look like a hero."

"I'm not."

"Then how did you get past the last Sister of Avalon? How did you make it to the Grey Isle?"

"Don't you mean, how do I plan to defeat you when it's fairly obvious that I do not fight?" I let my shadows loose, just a little, and the minotaur shuddered.

"We know full well you can kill me," he murmured. "But what will you endure in the process?"

"What I must."

I could tell that he didn't want to do this. He was trembling visibly when he lowered his head to charge at me. There was, I imagined, nothing he could do, though. This was his task, his curse, and the price of failing to perform it would be as bad as facing me. In that moment, I forgot that I was immortal, a primal force of the universe. I was sorry that I had power beyond what most people could conceive. I was sorry that I had the ability to destroy with a single touch. This wasn't fair. He didn't deserve this. He didn't deserve me.

The minotaur charged.

I reached out and brushed my hand over his aura again, plucking at the silver strand amongst the golden lifeforce. The minotaur's horns were inches from my face when I snapped that strand.

He let out a horrific scream and fell to the ground, writhing in agony. I crouched beside him and waited for the agony to pass, for the blinding pain to recede. Eventually, he calmed, breathing heavily, moaning and whimpering. He looked up at me, left pupil blown from the stress.

"I'm sorry," I said, and I was. "This isn't fair, not to you. But fairness is not my province. That belongs to Life. My province is death."

"Are you going to kill me now?" he rasped. I couldn't tell if he was begging me to do so, or to hold my hand.

"I've taken your immortality," I said. "In a way, I have killed you, though it is slower and longer than any death from a sword or axe."

Tears filled his eyes. "You killed me?"

I nodded. He burst into sobs, punctuated by the occasional cry of pain from whatever residual stress being made mortal caused. After a while, he clambered to his knees and made a sort of crawling motion in my direction. He did it again, and again, and I realised after a minute that he was *bowing*.

"What are you doing?" I demanded, recoiling.

"Thank you. Thank you." He said this over and over again, finally looking at me with tears in his bovine eyes. "My curse. You broke my curse."

It must have been contingent on his death, which I had provided, in a sense. I still wanted to know who had set this curse up, but I doubted it was something I would ever know. They were long gone, in all likelihood, leaving behind the product of their power. Three beings who had each gone mad in their own ways as they stayed behind to prove the mettle of countless heroes. I was tired of proving grounds. I was tired of people having to prove their worth based on arbitrary guidelines set up so long ago that the original reasons for those guidelines had been forgotten. I was tired of it all.

And with that weariness came anger.

"Stop grovelling," I said coldly. "I only did what was required of me."

"You saved me," the minotaur insisted.

"Regardless, I have no interest in your gratitude. I want only to retrieve what I came here for and free those I'm tasked with freeing." I stood and went to the niche where the cup and sword were, pointedly ignoring the pile of the dead in the corner. "Tell me about these."

"The cup of life," the minotaur said reverently. "It is said to be able to bestow eternal life on any who drink it, to heal all wounds. Some call it the holy grail, others just the cup. The Fisher King held guardianship over it for centuries, but it was taken from him and brought here when…well, they say it was when he became corrupted, but I think the cup may have been the cause of his corruption."

His madness.

"Why?"

"To be always in the presence of something that can heal your wounds that cause you constant pain? To never be able to touch it, to never drink from it? To be dependent on one who might come and be worthy enough to wield such a gift?" The minotaur shook his head. "It was a cruel curse. One with far-reaching consequences."

As a result of being so close to his deepest desires, the Fisher King had started devouring any who might be worthy instead, and perhaps more besides. Like Setar, innocent and good, just because he had the potential that might free the cup. The Fisher King had grown accustomed to his pain and so, in desperately wanting to be free of it, had instead started to lean on it.

I knew a lot of people like that. Those who were so used to their flaws, their struggles, that the thought of continuing on without them was almost painful to consider.

"What about the sword?" I had an inkling, since I

was basically traipsing through a bastardised Arthurian legend, but I wanted to be sure.

"It's not Excalibur, if that's what you mean," the minotaur said. "That lies in the hands of others. No, this sword is supposedly forged from the blade of a spear that pierced the side of a doomed god. It can kill the deathless and shatter the chains of blood, or so I've been told."

So not Excalibur. I peered at the blade, wondering what would happen if it pierced my heart, seeing as I was supposedly deathless. I touched the edge of the sword, but all it did was give me a paper cut. I felt no particular power, no energy, nothing.

"It looks like an ordinary sword to me," I said, frowning.

The minotaur shrugged. "I wouldn't know. I've seen heroes who have supposedly bested me in battle burst into flames as soon as they picked it up."

I quirked a brow. "Flames? Really? Seems a bit dramatic."

I grabbed the sword and, for a brief moment, held my breath. Nothing happened. I gave it an experimental wave with my extremely poor form. Again, nothing happened.

"I think it's just an ordinary sword," I said. The minotaur watched me carefully.

"Perhaps," he said, chewing over the word, "if that's what you believe, then that's what it is."

I swallowed a snort. If only things were so simple as being caused by belief magic, then I would have sorted this whole mess out a long time ago. No, this was a different situation entirely, and I had a feeling that I wouldn't much like what would come next.

Even so, I took the cup—this one *did* have power radiating from it—and shoved it haphazardly into my suit jacket pocket. As I removed the cup, the whole place began to shake. The minotaur flinched as the ceiling cracked and the ground rippled beneath our feet.

"Don't tell me we have to run all the way up those stairs," I said drily. Before he could answer, I felt the ground surge upwards. The cave, I realised, was being lifted to the surface. It was, finally, a useful part of this curse. Turning the cavern into a lift after successful completion of a mission.

The ceiling split after a few seconds, revealing a cloudless sky. When we emerged entirely, the rest of the cavern falling away into rubble amidst the ruins, I saw that the mist had receded on the island, leaving only the sight of shaggy grass, dead trees, and the furious expression on the ghost's face.

CHAPTER 15

"So you've done it, then." The ghost glided forwards, looking thunderous.

"I did what I was told to do," I retorted. I looked behind me, but the minotaur was gone, vanished with the mist. I wondered if that meant he had gained his freedom or was entirely gone from this world. I wasn't Death yet; I wasn't sure I would have felt it if he died.

"Do you even understand the consequences of your actions?" She swirled around me, looking me over. "Do you understand what will happen now that you have sword and cup?"

"Okay, first of all, this is just a regular sword," I said, waving the piece of metal around. "And secondly, *you* were the one who told me what to do.

You told me to go have my strength tested. You sent me down to where the minotaur lived and I did as you demanded."

She threw her hands up. "I didn't expect you to actually *do* it. To win."

Why did everyone have rules and expectations if they didn't actually believe people would follow them? I grinned, showing my teeth. "So I can see. You expected me to die, to end up in a pile of bone and weapons, like the others. Well, I haven't died. I've finished your little challenge."

"It was not meant for you," the ghost hissed. "It was meant for the chosen."

This was the first I was hearing of a particular chosen one. I hated dealing with prophecy and chosen one. There was always so much interpretation involved.

"This whole place is a proving ground for heroes," I said, waving my head in a wide sweep. "I've been told so many times. And yes, I grant you, I am not the hero you wanted or expected. I am no hero according to your ridiculous standards. Yet I have completed the challenges. I've broken the minotaur's curse. I have your sword and your cup. What more do you want from me?"

Honestly, I didn't have that much more to give.

The ghost let out a cry of frustration. "It's not

merely a matter of breaking the curses! It's a matter of what comes afterwards."

Ah, now we were getting somewhere. "What, exactly, comes afterwards?"

"The barriers fall."

"Barriers?" I frowned. "What barriers?"

The ghost just looked at me, expression inscrutable. I tried to puzzle together what she was talking about, and then it hit me. It was the only barrier that I had passed through to get here. I'd never once considered *why* the Fisher King and all this mess was located so far north, beyond even the dragon lands. I'd just thought it a coincidence. And then, when Casperion told me his version of the legends, how the dragons had reclaimed the scorched lands, how the Fisher King had been bound, I'd believed him.

A foolish thing, I realised now, given what had happened.

"The barriers to the dragon lands," I said. "They will fall when the curses are all broken? Surely, the dragons can pass between them already. I've seen them in the mortal realms. And there was an exile who—"

"Who *bound* them." The ghost twitched her skirts with a deft shake of her hand; they swirled around her ominously. I wondered how long she'd practised that.

"I've still seen them in the mortal realms." Just one, granted, but it had definitely been a dragon. Not to mention the fact that they'd been coming after my mother, and she was sure to know a dragon when she saw one.

"Dragons are realm breakers," the ghost said. "They can cross that barrier with ease. But here? In Elsewhere, the seat of their power? Why is it that no one has seen them beyond the dragon lands? These are beings who are both intelligent and powerful. Do you honestly think that they, out of all the beings in Elsewhere, are benevolent enough to keep to themselves and not interfere?"

"And Casperion, the exile, you're saying that—"

"A dragon alone could bind another dragon. It was done with a curse. One powerful enough to require a hero to break it." The ghost regarded me cooly. "Or whatever it is that you are."

Then he had told me more lies about the Fisher King, about all of this. I clenched my jaw. Too many lies. Too many conflicting stories. I wasn't sure who to believe, at this point, and I was getting tired of peeling back the layers of the story. I seized the part of the story I believed to actually be true.

"So, what, you and the others are trapped here because of a curse, which you would like broken. But if I break that curse, then the dragons are free to roam around Elsewhere without check? You seem to think this would be bad. What am I meant to do, then?" I hated these sorts of things. Do what you're asked and things end badly. Do nothing and things end badly. It was more than just a bad deal, it was infuriating.

"You must decide that for yourself," the ghost said, folding her hands in her skirts. She lifted her chin. "A true hero would walk away, a testament to their righteousness that they would rather fail than cause such havoc to fall upon the world."

"And we have already established that I'm no hero." I ran a hand through my hair. "Damn you. Damn the dragons. Damn them all."

Death surely knew about this curse and why the Fisher King was bound. How could he not? Yet he had sent me here anyways, demanding that I free the Reapers. He had known the consequences of defeating the Fisher King, of freeing the Reapers. He had known and deemed it acceptable, regardless.

"Do you know who sent the Reapers here?" I asked quietly, hoping that might give me some answers. "Who deemed them unsuitable for the world, or too powerful, or too precious to Life and Death and thus sent them to their doom?"

The ghost shook her head. "I do not. I deal only with the heroes that cross the lake, not those that the Fisher King devours before they can even make it this far."

Figured. I thrust the tip of the sword into the ground and paced a tight circle. Then, I paused. "What do you want?" I asked. "Out of all of this, what would you choose me to do?"

Her expression grew pained. "I am the last of my kind, the last Sister of Avalon. I have no kith nor kin and I cannot even know the peace of sleep or dreams. It is a cruel fate. Yet the consequences of breaking my curse…"

"Are for me to deal with," I said evenly. "I asked only what you wanted, not what would come afterwards."

She closed her eyes. "I would be free. Free to finally die, to pass on to whatever lies beyond." Her breath hitched and her eyes snapped open. "You are death-bound. What does lie beyond?"

I shook my head. "I do not know. I am bound to a moment, an act. Death. My power exists there, not beyond it."

"But…but you've seen it?" she asked, hopeful. "Even in the eyes of the dying?"

I thought of all those who had died by my touch. All those whose life had slipped from their eyes as I watched. I nodded. I had seen it, in the reflections that shone in their eyes.

"And?"

I drew the sword from the ground. It might not have any special powers, but it would serve as a tool for what I needed to do. I let my vision fade to grey, let the weak threads that lingered around her form come to the forefront of my vision. Then, in a move so swift that she could not have expected it, I severed those threads.

"It is beautiful," I said as the ghost faded away into nothing. "More beautiful than you can possibly know."

Damn the consequences, too.

I was done fixing things that other people had broken, putting the world back in order. I had seen what that life gave me, and it was nothing more than an office with an empty title. I was to become Death, and what was death if not change? Death of a thought, and a new one takes its place. Death of a time. Of a way of life. Of rules. It wasn't just life that ended, it was everything. Everything died.

And I was going to be there for all of it.

The island began to shake, gently at first, then more dramatically. The ground rent in a fissure that let the water of the lake drain downwards, emerging as poisonous steam that hissed with heat from underground fires. The few living plants on the island were destroyed, and the ruins eaten by the earth. The lake emptied, leaving a barren wasteland in its wake.

I hefted the sword over my shoulder and walked across the wasteland, ignoring the squelching in my shoes as the poisonous mud sucked at my soles. The distant shore approached faster than I expected, and soon I was faced with the Fisher King, looking hungrily at me, legs buried in mud.

"I didn't think you could do it." He licked his desiccated lips, showing his rotted teeth in a feral smile. "You, not even a hero."

"It seems your system was designed to fail, with the consequences of breaking the curse being to forever change the world," I retorted, stepping around him to get to the shore. He reached eagerly for the cup sticking out of my pocket; I danced out of his reach, patting the cup.

"That foolishness is none of my doing," he said. "Give me the cup. End my curse."

"Why should I?" I knew it would have to be done for no other reason than I needed to save Setar and the Reapers, and whoever else had been bound by his devouring nature. That didn't mean I couldn't make him pay, first. I could not kill him with my bare hands, but words were just as dangerous a weapon. Perhaps more so.

The Fisher King curled his lip. "Because it is your duty."

I laughed without humour. "My duty? Do you know what my duty is?"

He hesitated, shifting his feet in the mud, but still

unable to come any closer. "You want to save those that came before, those that I…took."

"Those whose potential you consumed in the hopes that it would restore you in a way that nothing else would. You tried to gain eternal life by stealing the life of others, but it didn't work." I patted my pocket with the cup again and he lunged for me, though the boundary of the shore held him back. "That's why they're still alive, why I never felt their deaths. They still exist in stasis, as you are in stasis, forever stuck in darkness. I know why the minotaur was cursed—he was one of the few who could test a hero's strength, consistently and without fail. And the ghost? The last Sister of Avalon, a land of mist and magic and dreams? I know why she was chosen, for where else could you find someone to test the righteousness and core of a person? But you? You're just a man, dead without dying, wounded without healing, stuck forever at this lake, able only to watch as it rots away. What in the world would cause someone to curse *you*?"

The Fisher King didn't tear his gaze away from the cup in my pocket, as if he was unable to do anything while it was near. Unable to think. Unable to reason. Unable to lie.

"I was cursed because I wanted what was not mine."

I reached into my pocket, the Fisher King's eyes

caught on my fingers. He gulped and swallowed when I drew the cup out, enraptured. "Wanted what, eternal life?"

"I wanted *power*. Eternal life means nothing without the power to influence, to control. I wanted power. I wanted knowledge. I wanted…" He spat on the ground, curling his lip. "I went to the wrong person with my desires, with my needs, and they laughed at me. For my insolence, I was told I could have the power over a kingdom of my own, the power to judge heroes who sought their own power. It was everything I thought I wanted. And what do I have instead? A barren, poisoned kingdom, a death that will never come, and no one worthy to take that cup from this place."

His eyes finally left the cup and moved to mine. There was cruelty there, and more. Madness. "As you are not worthy."

"Perhaps not," I said, "but it is mine all the same."

"I have nothing left but this curse, this power to hold back the dragons, to determine the worth of others. If you will not end my curse and give me the freedom I deserve, then I will have to exercise my power."

I scoffed. "And do what, exactly?"

"Kill you."

I very nearly laughed outright. "You are more than welcome to try."

The Fisher King pulled his feet from the mud and leaped for me, hands outstretched. I had only a moment to react before darkness, deeper than the void which was at my command, reached for and consumed me, bringing the sword and cup with it.

CHAPTER 16

When I opened my eyes, there was only emptiness around me. It wasn't the sort of emptiness I usually saw when I died and came back to life. That was vast and white and silent, like being blinded by the sun. This was darkness, the sort that lingered in the quietest hours of the night, only with no stars, no wind, nothing to break its hold. It wasn't the darkness of the end of things, or of sleep, or peace. It was just dark.

I turned around in a slow circle, wondering if my eyes would adjust. Perhaps I had been blinded and just couldn't see. I didn't think so, but it was a quiet hope. Eventually, I gave up on trying to see and started walking, thinking that I would run into something at some point.

Walking in pitch darkness was difficult. I kept

stumbling over my feet, even though I knew where they were. My hands were stretched before me to keep me from running into a wall or a tree or something, even though I expected no such thing in this place.

I should have expected it, though. I tripped over a smallish rock on the ground and fell onto my knees, yelping in pain. Almost immediately, I heard a rustling and a tiny snarl, then sparks filled the air and proved that I was definitely not blind.

The afterimage that imprinted itself on my eyes was small, cat-like, with a long neck and tail.

"Setar?" I asked.

"Cal!" the tiny dragon said. The next thing I knew, he had jumped head first into my middle, the dragon equivalent of a hug. I wrapped my arms around him, cradling him to me. He trembled fiercely, wings twitching and tail lashing. I made soothing noises, held him close, until finally, he settled. He let out a deep sigh. Calm.

"How did you get here?" the dragon hiccoughed. "I looked and looked and looked, but you weren't here. And what about Hester and Caris?"

"They're safe," I assured him. "They've gone back to your families."

"But…not me. I ended up here." Setar pushed his nose into the crook of my arm.

"Yes. We'll get out of this again, don't you worry."

"How?" The word was barely a whisper, hardly audible, yet it seemed to echo in this empty darkness. I didn't have an answer for the dragon. I had only annoyance with myself for not anticipating the Fisher King's attach, for not dodging him while I had the chance. Out there, I could tempt him and taunt him with the cup, with his freedom, until he gave me what I wanted. But in here?

"Setar, have you found anyone else?" I asked. I looked around and thought, maybe, that I was beginning to see something, even though I knew it was probably a trick of the light. Or dark, as it were. There wasn't any source of light, and there wasn't anything to shine the light on, so how could there be anything to see? Still, I fixed my gaze on the distant idea of a horizon and, standing with the dragon in my arms, started walking.

"No," Setar mewled. He curled tighter to me. "It was just darkness and silence. No warmth, no cold, just nothing. I…"

"It's okay," I assured him. "I've got you now. You're not alone."

"Promise?"

"Promise." I kept walking, something in me sure that I was going in the right direction. I didn't know how, or why, only that it was so. "We have to find some people, and then we can all get out of here."

He didn't repeat his earlier question, but I felt it

hanging in the air, nonetheless. How we were going to get out of this place was a mystery. Instead, I kept one hand on the dragon's back and started telling stories.

Stories about how I'd once been a petsitter for Death, and how his dogs had escaped, forcing me to go on an adventure through Faerie and get them back. Stories about how I'd travelled through time to provide relationship counselling for Life and Death before things could get really bad. Stories about Yolanda. About us eating popcorn and watching soap operas. Stories about Agravane, and his infuriating habit of doing everything just a little bit wrong to annoy me, even though his mistakes usually ended out well. Stories about Neja, and how we'd first met after she dropped a piano on me. Stories about Baz and the time we tricked the giants and angels to save the mortal realms.

None of my stories were about the life I led before, the life I had when I was human and unaware of the things that truly existed in the world. These were stories about my life, not about me fixing other people's lives.

I didn't regret my death, I realised as I told Setar stories about Charlotte the Unkillable and her time travelling journalist companion. I didn't regret being shot in the park. Not one bit.

I had blood on my hands, without a doubt. And

there were things about being human that I missed, but I was satisfied with my life as it was.

Well, there were a few things I needed to sort out, such as the Fisher King having trapped me in an eternal space of emptiness, and the fact that my mother and girlfriend were currently being held captive by dragons, but in general, things were good.

"Do you see that?" I asked, halfway through my story about how I arranged free coffee for life. "In the distance. Do you see that?"

My eyes were surely playing tricks on me. It looked like—

"A campfire!" Setar exclaimed. He sat up, neck stretched and eyes eager, and I realised that I could actually see him. He was still shadowed, mostly impossible to see against the black, but there was a distinct gleam to some of his scales that grew the closer we drew to the fire.

It wasn't a campfire, though, it was much, much larger than that. A bonfire, made of an impossible assortment of objects. A chair, straight out of my school days. A wardrobe that surely would take us to Narnia, a pile of what looked like priest's robes. These were at the outer edges of the fire, where they were barely starting to singe. The centre of the fire had similar items, almost entirely destroyed.

In a place of emptiness and darkness, this should have been impossible.

Then, I felt a dagger at my throat and felt much better about things. This made more sense than an unguarded bonfire of impossible things.

"Who are you?" a terse voice asked, rough and gravelly, likely from smoke inhalation. A second set of hands started patting me down, grabbing the sword from me and taking the cup from my pocket. Setar hissed when the hands got too close to his perch on my arm, and they hesitated.

"Tad, that's a dragon." This voice was female, also rough from smoke, but much younger than the other voice. I turned my head a fraction and received a snarl from Tad.

"Don't move."

"Alright," I said. Setar hissed at the woman as she reached for him.

"I won't leave Cal!" he squeaked, swiping at her with minuscule claws. She pulled back, and I finally got a good look at her.

Thin and ragged, she was Black and wore the tattered remnants of robes that were at least two sizes too big for her. Her feet were bare and her hair unkempt. There was a wild light in her eyes that worried me, especially considering it was directed at Setar.

"Cal, eh?" Tad asked, stepping around me, knife still held at my throat. He finally stood in front of me, back to the fire, dagger gleaming in the light. He looked as ragged as the woman. With olive skin and dark hair that was too scraggly to be fashionable, features that were too thin to be healthy, and that same wild look in his eyes, I half expected him to throw the dagger at me. Instead, he handed the sword to the woman and fingered the stem of the cup.

"Who are you?" he asked again, curling his lips in a snarl.

"I'm Cal Thorpe," I said, and peered closer at these two. "On the off chance you're Reapers, I'd like to inform you that I work for Death."

That was, apparently, the wrong thing to say. Tad threw the knife just as the woman thrust at me with the sword. Both hit at precisely the same moment, one to the throat and the other to my heart. I gagged, gasped for half a second, then fell to the ground. My vision flashed white, leaving my eyes with a horrible afterimage in this dark place, the fire basically blinding me when I opened them again.

"Seriously?" I demanded once I could see again. Groaning, I tried to sit up, but there was a weight on my chest. Setar. He stood there, claws dug into my shirt, maw opened and sparks flaring.

"Don't you touch him!" the dragon cried, voice cracking. "You killed him!"

"Setar," I said, reaching up and touching the dragon. He jumped and yelped, spinning around. His eyes widened as he saw me moving, the wounds healed.

"Cal?"

"I'm okay, buddy. Truly."

"Impossible," the woman said, gaping at me. "I killed you."

"Yeah, thanks for that. It hurts, you know, getting killed." I raised myself to my elbows and received a nuzzle from Setar for my trouble. He was still trembling, but it was reduced. I sat up entirely and caught the dragon in my arms. "Hey, it's alright," I murmured. "You're going to be okay."

The dragon child nodded and crawled onto my shoulder, burying his head against my neck. I stood, dusted myself off, and finally turned to my would-be murderers, the full force of my displeasure in my glare. Tad backed away while the woman raised my sword again, hands wavering.

I straightened my suit. "Perhaps we should start again," I said darkly. "I am Cal Thorpe. I am a Reaper, who stands at the crossroads of choice. Within my chest, I have the heart of the end of all things. I am to be Death, when he ventures into the void. Who, then, are you?"

Tad's left eye twitched. "I am Thaddeus of Filleni, Reaper who stands at the precipice of change."

"I am Iliana, Reaper who stands beside the momentous." She sketched a sarcastic bow, though I could tell there was real fear in her eyes. "How did you…how can you be…" She looked away.

"I took a job with Death some few years ago, and since then have discovered that I am a Reaper—the last, we all thought. There were a few mishaps with my soul, and some blood magic, and well, I ended up as heir to Death." I modulated my tone; it wasn't these people's fault that they were scared, defensive. "I discovered that the other Reapers weren't dead, but trapped, and Death sent me here to find you."

"Death sent you here," Iliana said, choking out a laugh.

"Yes."

"After all this time." She abruptly turned away and ran to the far side of the bonfire, clutching her sides as she either laughed or sobbed hysterically. I turned to Tad, brows raised.

"You must excuse her. It has been a very, very long time since we were trapped here. We gave up hope a long time ago, after the rest of us died."

"There were more of you?" I had no idea how many Reapers there were meant to be, but I never figured there would be many. Just more than me.

"Twelve in total. Now it's just the three of us, if you'll let me include you in that number." Tad patted his ragged robes. He spoke again before I could ask my question. "We came to the dragon lands to investigate allegations that Knights were attacking without provocation. Some small source had whispered it in another small source's ears until the rumour had spread through Elsewhere like wildfire. You know the sort of thing."

I nodded. These things were now managed with social media, and they pretty much all came through my office, but the principle was the same. There was little chance of figuring out who started the rumour. Little chance of figuring out who tricked the Reapers.

"We came here and found nothing amiss with the dragons. They asked us to see if anything could be done about the Fisher King, about the boundaries on their lands, and we promised to investigate. We were the only ones who could, you see, given the particular nature of the curse." Tad scowled, glaring at the fire. "It was a mistake. A trap. The first of our order perished before we were even fully bound here, trying to reverse our steps. The others died of attrition, or they wandered into the black and never returned, their bodies appearing only weeks later. We managed to collect detritus and create this bonfire, this beacon, but...we're almost out of supplies. This place is empty and hasn't been renewed for centuries."

"Was it the dragons who tricked you here, do you think?" Why they would want the Reapers gone, I had no idea.

Tad shook his head. "No. Yes. Perhaps. I don't know, and I've thought it over a thousand times. We were led here by the lone dragon who exists outside the bounds of their lands. He was the one who suggested we help them."

I wanted to scream at myself for being such a trusting idiot. Instead, I shoved my hands into my pockets. "His name wouldn't happen to be Casperion, would it?"

CHAPTER 17

At the sound of the dragon's name, Setar sprang up from my neck and hissed violently, scales rattling, sparks flying. A couple landed on my skin and I winced. Tad took a step back, flicking his gaze to where Iliana was still hunched over by the fire. She appeared to be listening, but unable to do anything but sit there, rocking gently back and forth. Frankly, I couldn't blame her.

"Relax," I snapped, plucking Setar from my shoulder and holding him at a distance. He wriggled in my grasp.

"No! No! Not until you tell me how you know the traitor!" The young dragon was vehement, furious, the most I'd seen from him. All traces of fear were gone, replaced by the sort of anger that would tear down worlds.

As quickly as possible, I explained how my mother, Neja and I had met Casperion on the road, the things that he promised to help us with, the bargain that we made. I explained his obvious treachery to the other dragons, and to me, and how I had released him from the bargain and he had run off. Setar hissed at significant points of the story, but calmed down when he realised I wasn't conspiring with the older dragon.

"We knew nothing of his treachery against the other dragons," Tad said, "only that he directed us here, that he suggested we could help by breaking the curse. Obviously, he wanted the boundaries down for his own benefit."

"He is a traitor," Setar snarled, claws digging into my skin. I yelped and nearly dropped the dragon. I set him down instead, letting the black youngling pace his fury out. He did so, tail twitching, tiny wings furling and unfurling. Finally, he stopped, unable to contain his emotions any longer, and let out a desperate sob. "He k-killed my father!"

Tad and I exchanged a glance and then sat on the ground, the dragon between us. Setar climbed into my lap, crying fiercely.

"W-when he wasn't allowed to lead, despite being the oldest, h-he called all the dragons together and suggested a summit to determine the leader, and then he did a great magic to bind everyone to this place, but it went wrong somehow and a b-bunch of the big dragons were killed when they tried to stop it and…and…" Setar broke off in a loud wail that echoed eerily in this empty place.

"Hush, little one," I soothed as best I could, brushing my fingers along his spine like I did with Tempest, my pet. As it did with her, the touch settled the small dragon.

"My mother hatched me from her last clutch," Setar said. "She waited centuries to do it. Said she wanted it to be the right time."

Dragon eggs were viable for countless generations and often fiercely protected, given how few of them there were. I had only ever encountered them once, but the dragon sent to retrieve them would have had no qualms about tearing open the world to protect those eggs. I wondered if the dragon I had met had been related to Setar, if I had once protected his egg.

"It seems to me," I said slowly, still stroking the dragon, "that the best thing to do would be to call Casperion out. To demand recompense. Justice."

If I'd had my phone, I would call Baz. He could surely take some time off from his expedition to America to help with a crime against all the dragons. As it was, my phone was in a bag on the ground at the feet of the Fisher King. I'd have to escape to actually do anything. And, frankly, this was one thing that I wanted to do myself. This was personal.

Casperion had lied to me, had betrayed me and mine, and had harmed this child. My mother and Neja were in the custody of dragons because of him. The minotaur and ghost and Fisher King had been bound in endless torment because of him. Obviously, the dragons hadn't wanted to do more than run him off, perhaps for sentiment or past favours or something. I had no such compunctions.

"That's all well and good," Iliana said, crawling over to us, eyes crazed. "Except for the part where we're trapped here."

I winced. Yes, well. There was that.

"I assume you've explored this place as far as you can?"

Tad and Iliana gave me a flat look. "As far as the horizon stretches," Tad said in disgust. "We found nothing but dead bodies of those who could not take the emptiness, and random…objects that the Fisher King devoured by accident."

"The modern word is 'stuff', if you're wondering," I offered, reminding myself that these people had been out of the world for centuries. They would have no idea about modern slang or social media or even coffee.

"I wasn't," Tad snapped.

"Alright, there's no visible exit," I said, changing

the subject. "What about trying to break this place by force?"

"What do you mean?"

I let some of my shadows bleed into my skin, my form flickering for a moment into the being of coils and claws and a maw of deadly fangs. Tad reared back and Iliana cursed.

"What?" I frowned. I had assumed that all Reapers had a secondary form, one used when at the height of their power. Was I wrong?

"You...that's..." Tad rubbed the back of his neck.

"You're stupidly powerful," Iliana said evenly. "I can change to a dog, and only a small hound at that, and Tad is—"

"A bear," he said, sounding almost rueful.

"But you?" Iliana shook her head. "No wonder you ended up as Death's heir."

"Right." Even with immortality now running through my veins, it occasionally unsettled me to learn of such things. To learn that I wasn't typical or normal. Then again, when had I ever been such a thing? I closed my eyes and sighed. "So I take it you can't rip this place apart with your other shapes?"

Both Reapers shook their heads.

"I was worried about that. I physically tore the Fisher King to pieces and received nothing for my efforts. Just a directive to fetch the cup and, apparently, that sword." I nodded at the sword by Iliana's side.

"It's just a sword," she said, frowning in confusion.

"That's what I thought." I wasn't sure why everyone was so concerned with a plain sword. Yes, I'd used it to kill that ghost, but only as an extension of my own power, nothing more. "The Fisher King was more concerned with the cup, anyhow."

Tad looked around and picked up the cup where it had fallen during the various adventures of me being killed and them freaking out at me. In the fire-light, it looked like nothing more than an old, worn goblet, hardly enough for three mouthfuls of wine or water or whatever. I know in some legends, this was the holy grail, the cup Jesus Christ drank from at the last supper. In other legends, it was a cauldron. The cup of life.

"Foolish man swallowed it instead of letting me have it," I said as Tad held it up to the light.

"It won't mean much in this place. We are already eternal here. This is a place of in betweens. Neither here nor there. Neither alive nor dead. Neither—"

"In betweens?" I asked. In betweens was where my power was at its best. It was where *all* Reapers existed. In between Life and Death and everything else. It was, perhaps, why, out of all the beings that the Fisher King had devoured, only Reapers remained.

Iliana caught on first. "We should be able to manipulate this place. Choose."

Tad shrugged his rags closer to his body. "The others chose, Iliana. Look what it got them: us burning their bodies because there was no other source of fuel."

I winced at that. Even as we'd been sitting here, the bonfire was eating through the last pieces of furniture on the fire, and I doubted very much that more would be forthcoming. Not with the cup and sword in my possession. No other heroes would come here. Once the fire burned out, that was it.

"They chose to die," Iliana said, nodding eagerly. She crawled towards me, that desperate madness tingeing her voice. She giggled. "We can choose to live."

I didn't think it would be *quite* that easy, given that they'd been living here all this time and were still trapped. But there was a way to find out. "Pull the wardrobe out of the fire," I instructed.

Without hesitation, Tad leaped to his feet and started wrestling the piece of furniture from the fire. It had started to smoke quite seriously, and there were a few pieces at the very top that had caught and were smouldering, but it was still relatively whole. The door swung open, revealing that the back panel was almost entirely burned through, but I didn't think that it mattered. It was the door that was important.

"What next?" Tad asked, a little too eagerly. He, too, was likely mad from being here for so long, but he hid it better than his companion. She showed it in look and movement. He showed it in eagerness, in word. I wondered what their reaction would be to returning to the world, then mentally shook myself. I didn't have time for wondering. I needed to act.

"Well, I don't think it's going to be quite as easy as, say, us choosing to step through that door and find ourselves back at the lake's edge." I stood and went to the door of the wardrobe, wincing at the residual heat in the wood. I closed my eyes, thought of the drained lake and the furious Fisher King, and decided that would be my reality. I even invoked my Reaper powers, letting colour fade from my vision and shadows leap and writhe around me. Then, I opened the door.

The bonfire leapt for me, as if eager to reclaim the fuel taken from it. I sighed and closed the wardrobe door again.

"Then it's hopeless," Iliana said, bottom lip wavering, tears filling her eyes. She started trembling.

"No. Not hopeless. Just more difficult." Tension gathered in my shoulders when I thought about what I had to do next. It wasn't going to be good or pretty or even kind. But it was the only way I could think to make this work.

I turned to Setar, sitting on the ground where I had been sitting, looking confused. He likely didn't understand the discussion of our Reaper abilities, or what we intended. It was better that way, because if he did understand, then this probably wouldn't work.

"Setar," I said, kneeling before him. He looked up at me with such hope, with such eagerness. "You do not belong to this place like the Reapers do."

"I don't?" he chirped, tail twitching.

"No." My human form started to fall away, pieces of me shedding and being replaced with shadow. My voice grew deeper, my vision darker. "Your presence here is interferring with the place of in betweens. You do not belong in between. You belong to a world of life. Or—" and here, I let my human shape fall away entirely, stretching my head up and revealing fangs and claws and terrible coils, "—a world of death."

Setar gaped at me in horror. "C-Cal?" he whispered, visibly shaking.

"I've figured it out, see?" I said, wrapping my coils around him. Tad and Iliana caught on, shedding their shapes, too, revealing a shaggy black dog and a bear with massive shoulders and claws that could easily rend flesh, each creatures of the blackest void. "It's the *others* that made this place continue to exist. To keep us trapped here. Those who are not Reapers. Who belong in one or the other. As you do."

Setar whimpered, trying to follow both Iliana and Tad as they circled him, glowing golden and orange eyes fixated on the little dragon. He cowered down, flattening to the ground as best he could. I twined my coils closer, dropping my head to him.

"Since you have been a good companion," I crooned, "I am going to give you a choice. Live, and go through that door there to the world whence you came. Or die by my claws."

I desperately hoped he chose to live, because if he chose otherwise, then not only would he be dead, but I would be the one to do it. I was immortal, with no humanity left in me, but killing children was not something I ever believed I would enjoy. It was a waste, and nothing could convince me otherwise.

I bared my fangs at Setar. He let out a low keening sound, his scales rattling, his eyes screwed shut. I realised a moment later that he was crying. My instinct was to comfort him, to make him understand that everything would be alright, but I couldn't.

I could only wait for him to choose.

CHAPTER 18

"W-why are you doing this?" Setar sobbed, turning in a quick circle to watch Tad and Iliana circle around him again. I rattled my coils and he sank flatter to the ground, wings tight against his back.

"Because I must," I growled, drawing close enough so that he could see my eyes, see my fangs, see how serious I was.

"Please," he begged. "Please."

"Choose," I snapped, clicking my teeth. "Life in the world that you know, or death, here, at my claws."

Setar flinched as I showed him those claws. I gestured to the door and he eyed is longingly. "Y-you won't hurt my family if I choose to go back?" he asked, voice no more than a whisper. My heart broke a little more. He had already lost his father at the hands of someone who betrayed his family, and here he was, thinking that I was doing the same. Betraying him.

"Your family will be safe from me," I said. "My interest is only in you at the moment."

He let out another keening sound. Iliana snapped her jaws in frustration, impatience getting the better of her.

"Choose, dragon!" she snarled, a rumbling growl building in her throat. Tad copied her, his bear's shape making the sound echo into a roar. Setar buried his snout in his forepaws.

"I choose the other world!" he cried.

The three of us Reapers quickly took human form again, though my shadows still swarmed over my skin, and my vision was still colourless. The door of the wardrobe, which had begun to smoulder, despite having us pulled it from the fire, started to rattle. I leaned over, picked up Setar, who squirmed and squealed and kicked.

"Calm yourself," I said, though I doubted it would help. "The choice has been made. See now what your decision has wrought."

Tad opened the door, which showed a sliver of light that didn't belong in this empty place, and slipped through, Iliana close on his tail. Setar pulled back, then squeezed his eyes shut and dug his claws into my hand as I stepped through the door.

The world changed shape in a rush of colour and sound. The poisoned lakeside rematerialised, exactly as it had been, including the Fisher King standing stuck in mud. The two Reapers were some small distance off, touching the ground and blinking rapidly as their eyes adjusted to the light of the real world after so long in emptiness. Setar was suddenly still, staring at the lake, at the dragon lands in the distance.

"You saved us," I whispered to the dragon. He flinched and looked up at me in surprise. "Thank you."

Understanding dawned and emotions played across his features until he settled on a small smile and a nod. "You're welcome," he said, voice quiet. Then, he wriggled again and jumped from my arms, galloping off towards the lush dragon lands without a backwards glance.

I rubbed a spot on my hand where his claws had caught, watching him go. When he was no more than a black dot in the grass, I picked up the sword that Iliana had dropped as soon as she emerged from the shadows. I took the cup in my other hand, then faced the Fisher King.

He watched with the wariness of prey cornered by a much larger predator. His tongue darted out and licked cracked, desiccated lips. He smiled, rotted teeth showing. "You...you escaped."

I hummed softly in my throat. "Did you think that I would not?"

He didn't answer.

"Foolish man." I held up the cup and the sword. "You devoured the very thing that would break your curse. Have you grown so used to your powerless immortality that even the thought of freedom was poison to you?"

"Powerless?" The Fisher King scoffed. "I have more power than you could imagine."

I clicked my tongue. "Oh, yes. The power to decide heroes. To keep the dragons bound. All for the price of your health, your freedom. Tell me: was it worth it?"

He shifted in the mud, wincing at the squelching sound. I took a step forwards. He retreated.

"Just as I offered a choice to the child you devoured in your quest for power that was not yours, I will offer you a choice." I looked at him again, with my Reaper eyes. As before, there was swirling emptiness around him, but in between and throughout that nothingness were the specks of silver and sickly yellow that I sought.

"A choice?" He sounded relieved.

"The cup, or the sword." I lifted each in turn.

He frowned, the movement drawing unnatural

lines on his broken skin. "What?"

"Your end. Will it be by cup, or by sword?"

"T-that's no choice at all! You can't tell me that I will meet my end and expect that picking one method or the other will make up for taking away my chance to live!"

I bared my teeth at him. "I am a Reaper. I am the giver of choice, the one who stands between. I am the master of crossroads and all choice is mine to rule."

"That's not fair!" he screamed, the cry echoing across the lake.

I grinned. "Life's not fair, dear King. Surely you knew that already."

The Fisher King shook his head. "No. I choose to live."

"Then you should have done differently before now." I took another step forwards. "The choice before you is to meet your end by either the cup, or the sword. You can do so with dignity, or with terror. I do not mind, either way, though I have no doubt that my associates would prefer to see you trembling."

Iliana and Tad were, indeed, recovering their sense of reality and were turning towards me. They saw what I was doing, and I saw an eager glint in both their eyes. Vengeance, in so far as a Reaper could deliver such a thing.

The Fisher King flinched and tried retreating, but the mud held fast, sucking at his feet and making certain he did not escape the choosing. He hunched his shoulders and tried appealing to my better nature. "You don't understand what you're doing," he said. "My being here is all that keeps the dragons contained. Would you deliver Elsewhere to them? To their whims and judgements?"

I laughed humourlessly. "I have already made that decision. The minotaur and the ghost both asked me the same thing. The consequences are *mine* and I accept them. Willingly. Just as you should accept your end."

He shook his head. "No. I won't accept it."

"If you refuse to choose, it will be both," I said, lifting my hands and the objects within them. "I have no interest in spending eternity waiting for you."

"You can't do this!"

"You'll find that he can," Iliana giggled. "The heir to Death and a Reaper of his power? He can do almost anything."

The Fisher King blanched, what little his decayed state could manage. "Heir to…" He hadn't realised before. He knew, certainly, about my being a Reaper as I had torn him apart in that form. But I hadn't said that Death's heart beat in my chest. I hadn't told him about what fate awaited me in the future. It wasn't any of his business, frankly, and I would admit that the fear people displayed at learning this news was annoying. Useful, perhaps, but annoying.

"Make your choice, Majesty," I hissed.

Tad stepped up to my right shoulder, eyeing the sword eagerly. Iliana appeared at my other side. The Fisher King looked between them desperately. Then, he grew still.

I saw the exact moment that resignation outweighed desperation. I saw the moment that he realised that his end was upon him and accepted it. His shoulders slumped, his head hung, and he seemed to collapse in on himself.

"It's been so long," he said, "since I was a man. Since I knew what it was to feel whole and hale. Since I knew anything but the edges of this poisoned place and the limitations of my worthless body."

He fell to his knees, defeated. "I'm tired," he murmured.

"I know." He wouldn't have asked me to end his curse otherwise. He would have devoured me instead of letting me cross the lake. The final result may have been the same, but it might not. He had started the process of his own ending and he knew it. Now, he accepted it.

"The cup or the sword?" I asked again, more gently.

With a trembling hand, he pointed to the cup. I handed the sword to Tad and stepped forwards with the cup. I knelt before the Fisher King, ignoring the mud that seeped instantly into the knees of my trousers. There was, to my left, a tiny puddle. Trapped between slightly higher points of the lake, it was all that remained of the water that had been here. I dipped the cup into the puddle and lifted the brackish water.

As I watched, it steamed in the cup, bubbling and frothing like a science experiment gone wrong. In another instant, the water cleared, appearing as pure as it could be. The cup of life indeed.

I handed the cup to the Fisher King, who tilted his face up, mouth open. The image reminded me of a medieval peasant waiting for the bread and wine from the priest of a church. Somehow beseeching and expecting at the same time. A last rite, perhaps the only rite he had ever known.

I obliged.

Tilting the cup, I dribbled water into his waiting mouth. He swallowed and closed his eyes, a moment of pleasure crossing his features. Of peace.

Then, his expression morphed into agony.

His skin rippled and twisted, swelling before my very eyes. In moments, he was human again. Skin fresh, smooth, eyes bright and clear. He blinked at me, astonished, then doubled over, clutching his stomach. His skin wrinkled and sagged, his hair grew grey, then white. His bones showed through his weak flesh. He aged, feeling every century that he had stood here guarding the lake.

He aged, and he died.

Bones replaced what had once been a man. The mud of the lake absorbed them with surprising alacrity, the remains of the poison dissolving the bone until it was nothing. I stood, watching the lake bed dry up until all evidence that there was ever a lake there disappeared.

"The sword would have been the faster death, I think," Tad said, curling his lip in disgust as grasses and flowers started crawling forwards, growing magically over the spot. In minutes, it was nothing more than a pleasant field, remnant of the rest of the dragon lands. All evidence of a curse, gone.

"Faster, yes. And kinder, too," I said, tucking the cup back into my pocket. "Life can be quite cruel, and I don't imagine her cup is any less so."

"He deserved it," Iliana said, spitting on the ground.

She turned to march away from the lake when I felt the entire realm shudder. It wasn't like an earthquake, where there was a physical manifestation of the turmoil beneath. Nor was it a storm, with winds and rain. It was physical, yes, but it was also mental, a scream in the mind.

All three of us staggered, clutching our ears and trying our best to keep upright. Iliana and Tad leaned on each other, a bond forged in darkness that was difficult to break. I leaned on the sword, hoping that it wouldn't break beneath me.

The sound stopped and we were left panting, sweating, reeling.

"What was that?" Tad demanded.

"That was the barriers breaking down," Iliana said. "Right, Cal? The barriers to the dragon lands? The ones that the Fisher King warned us about?"

I nodded. "I think so."

"This is bad, right?" Tad asked, eyes flashing skywards as though he expected dragons to start flocking overhead, screaming for their freedom.

"Probably."

"Well, what are you going to do about it?" Iliana demanded. Right, because everything was up to me.

I adjusted my glasses and tried to regain my bearings. It was up to me, not only in part because I had been the one to claim the consequences of my actions. It was up to me because the dragons, for all their new horizons, still had my mother and Neja captive. And, rules be damned, I wasn't going to let that stand.

"We start walking," I said. "This way."

I picked up the sword, hoisted it over my shoulder and began to march back into the depths of the dragon lands. The other Reapers followed behind, silent.

CHAPTER 19

It's difficult to keep up a good head of steam and rage when walking through an idyllic pre-industrialisation Italian countryside. Even Iliana and Tad had grown noticeably calmer during our trek, taking note of the trees and the meadows, wondering at the water. I had pulled out the remains of my supplied from my pack, which I'd grabbed upon our leaving the remains of the Fisher King's kingdom behind; Tad and Iliana devoured the rations like starving people. To be fair, they likely hadn't eaten in centuries.

The journey back to the entrance of the dragon lands felt a lot quicker than it had heading towards the ridiculous proving ground. We didn't have to stop overnight, and nor did we even pause for a meal or a break. Five-ish hours of walking—still hard on the feet, but that's what I get for walking around with mud-saturated shoes—and I spotted the roofless tavern.

There were, unsurprisingly, dragons congregating outside.

One of them was the elderly dragon I sought. She was snarling viciously at a younger dragon who looked decidedly agitated. When the others spotted myself and the two other Reapers cresting the hill, they all fell silent and stared.

I waved the sword at them in greeting. "Ciao," I said sweetly, dangerously. I was wrong. Even after all that walking, I was perfectly able to summon up a good mad. Perfect. I would need it.

"My lord," the leader of the dragons rasped. "You…You have returned."

"Haven't I just," I said. "It turned out that this whole Fisher King nonsense was a testing ground for heroes, and more than that, it was all some elaborate curse to contain the cup of life and this sword, for reasons I still can't figure out, as well as keep *you* contained."

The dragons shuffled uneasily. Some of the larger ones flared their wings as though they planned to strike. Beside me, Iliana's form flickered into that of the black dog and she let out a snarl. The dragons recoiled in shock.

"Oh, and did I mention, I found the Reapers, too,"

I said, smiling. "May I introduce Iliana, the wolf who would happily tear you all to shreds there. And Thaddeus, who shows a little more restraint, despite having been in captivity for centuries, but who I assure you is quite capable of violence."

Silence lay heavy between us. Eventually, the elder dragon took a hesitant step forwards. It was more of a shuffle, but it broke up the even line the dragons held against me. She eyed me warily, scales rattling slightly. Having experienced the young dragons, I now knew that to be a sign of fear.

"What is it you want, my lord?" she asked, tongue flicking out to taste the air. To taste my scent. My intentions.

"I want the return of what's mine." I plunged the sword into the earth. "As you are all well aware, the boundaries around this place are gone. You have the freedom of Elsewhere, now, but I think you already knew that. I think that knew full well what my breaking of the Fisher King's curse meant."

"It was not a secret," a young, golden dragon hissed, flaring a ruff behind his neck. "That we were bound here. That we were betrayed."

"Indeed," I said, nodding. "Casperion. The blue dragon who brought me here. Who asked only that I bring him through the barrier and keep him from my mother in exchange."

The golden dragon lashed his tail, but said nothing. The elder dragon shot him a look and he backed down, lowering his head. "The traitor, yes," she said, reasserting her authority with a puff of smoke.

"The traitor." I rolled the word around my mouth. "Iliana. Tad. What would *you* do if you came across a traitor who had imprisoned you, bound you, and then returned despite being exiled?"

Iliana snarled wordlessly, gnashing her void-dark teeth together. Tad nodded agreement. "Death would be swift," he said. "And merciless."

"Swift and merciless death," I mused. Turning back to the dragons, I tapped my chin in exaggerated confusion. "See, to me, and to everything in Elsewhere, that sounds quite reasonable. My cousin, who fills the role of Justice, wouldn't even disagree with me. Which then brings up the question of why you, who are much vaunted as being without hesitation to deal swiftly to those who harmed you, did nothing but watch Casperion run away."

The elder dragon turned to whisper to the others. A small, sleek green dragon with two sets of wings leaped into the air and streaked off, likely to fetch reinforcements. I hoped they would bring Mother and Neja back, too, or I was going to have to make myself difficult.

I wandered over to a nearby bench and sat, brushing off some of the dirt and grime of travel. The dragons watched me warily, shifting as I stretched. I held up a finger. "See, here's the thing. This whole thing, getting into the dragon lands, finding the Fisher King, retrieving the cup and sword, rescuing the Reapers, all of it, has been far more annoying than it should have been. I am deathless! I have dealt with the Fae countless times. I have battled rock trolls. I have acted on behalf of Life and Death in more ways than you could possibly know. I have died and been returned in many painful, memorable ways. I am, perhaps, not as knowledgeable regarding all the minute subtleties of Elsewhere politicking, but I am not a fool. So why was this particular quest so difficult?"

No one spoke. Iliana paced, snarling at any dragon who looked at her wrong. Tad remained standing sentinel by my side, intense glare fixed on the line of massive reptiles. Intelligent reptiles who breathed fire, could split the lines between realms in two, and claw me to tiny pieces without much effort. Intelligent reptiles who stood perfectly still, as prey faced a predator.

I sighed dramatically. "I see I'm going to have to explain everything. Casperion bound you, yes, and was exiled for it. But *my* theory is that he did so at your request. You grew afraid of dying, of losing any more than you already had. After all, you asked me for true immortality, and that is not a thing that long-lived ones such as you ask for when you are faced with an idyllic world like this. No one to hunt you, no one to hurt you, just dragons together in a utopian world."

The elder dragon shuffled her claws. I leaned forwards, shoving my glasses up my nose, and grinned viciously. "You wanted the barrier. You wanted to keep the rest of Elsewhere out. You wanted to protect yourselves from those who would willingly go toe-to-toe with a dragon in their pursuit of power. The Knights were almost extinct, but they were not the only threats to you, even if they were the most prominent. You locked yourselves in this world because you were *afraid*, didn't you?"

After a quick glance at her people, the elder dragon bobbed her head in a silent "yes."

"And you locked Casperion out because he was the one who bound you, didn't you?"

Another nod.

"You couldn't have him coming back for fear that his connection with the curse that kept everyone else out would mean the barriers weakened. You willingly sacrificed him to the outside world so you could have your happy little idyll." I scoffed and shook my head. "No wonder he wanted revenge. No wonder he kept sending heroes, people of power, to go and seek the Fisher King to try and break the curse. It wasn't his presence that let us through the barrier, it was the fact that there were potential heroes in my party. Not me, obviously, but the djinn? My mother? Both are brimming with self-sacrificing heroic potential."

I frowned. "Actually, my mother is not so much about self-sacrifice, but the point still stands."

"You brought Casperion back," the elder dragon snarled. "You let him back in."

I laughed drily. "Oh, I did much worse than that. I broke your curse. You're free. Ta da."

As I spoke those words, three things happened.

One, the green dragon who had flown off earlier returned with Tesana, the massive roof-removing dragon behind them. In Tesana's claws were my mother and Neja, both looking the worse for wear. Neja's nose was definitely broken, her eyes swollen and discoloured around the bent appendage. She had swelling on her knuckles, too, and I was all but certain that under her dark clothes, she had other bruises and scratches. My mother didn't have any visible injuries, but her hair was mussed into a rat's nest, her movie-style archaeologist's clothes were torn beyond repair, and she was missing a shoe.

Two, I could feel magic gathering around the dragons on the ground. The world began to shake from the force of the power. I didn't think that they would actively tear the realm apart right then, but they were afraid, and that could lead even the most sane people into trouble.

Three, I was attacked by two small creatures, a third one lingering not far from the others. Caris and Hester barrelled into me at speed, Caris landing on my lap and Hester running head-first into my leg. She quickly recovered and shook herself off, then climbed up my trousers to settle on my lap as well. Setar, still nervous of me after all that had happened, crawled a little closer, though he didn't get close enough to touch.

"Cal! You're back! You saved Setar!" Caris cried, nuzzling my chin.

Hester bounced excitedly. "He told us all about what happened with the empty place and the shadow magic and the choice that saved everyone. It must have been so exciting!"

"I'm not sure exciting was the word," I said, running my fingers down her spine. She arched and rubbed her head against my hand.

The dragons stared at me in abject horror at the sight of their children playing with someone they considered their enemy. A medium grey dragon inched forwards.

"Hester, Setar, Caris," she crooned, wings pressed tightly against her back. "Why don't you come play over here?"

"But we want to play with Cal!" Caris announced, trumpeting her annoyance with a burst of sparks. "He's fun."

"Children!" the dragon snapped. "Come here at once!"

The three young dragons froze and gaped at each other, and at me. I helped them off my lap and shooed them towards the adults. "Go one, now. We don't want to get you in trouble."

"Bye, Cal," Setar whispered, then slunk off after the other two.

Once the children had reached the grey dragon, she bundled them in her claws and took to the skies, vanishing in the blink of an eye. The elder dragon narrowed her eyes at me. "Why?" she hissed.

"I have no desire to harm children. They deserve no pain." I stood and brushed off my suit. "Yet children always seem to pay for the mistakes of others."

I thought of my payment for the mistakes of my father. Of Yolanda, who should have been a queen amongst her people, paying for the mistakes of *her* parents. Of all the Setars and Hesters and Carises who grew up too fast.

"What do you want, *Cal?*" the elder dragon asked.

"I can understand fear," I said. "I understand what it's like to be confronted by those who wish to kill you."

I had been human, after all, in a realm that thought humans were more plaything than creatures with rights.

"I can understand, even, locking yourself away

from the rest of the world based on that fear. I have no desire to punish you for that. The problem I'm having is that you involved innocents in your fear. Your curse was a hero's proving ground. A place where they either died or failed and were devoured by the Fisher King. You brought the Reapers into this mess, thus involving me."

"So you will kill us, then, Heir to Death?"

I shook my head. "No."

I lifted my sword over my shoulder and went to my mother and Neja, loomed over by Tesana. With one look from me, she retreated, hunching her shoulders. Neja ran to my arms in a surprising gesture of affection.

"You came for me," she said with a sniff and a wince about her broken nose.

"Of course I did. I can't believe you would doubt me!"

That earned me a punch in the shoulder.

"Calvin." My mother stepped forwards, arms wrapped around herself. Her family sword had been taken and her mouth twisted at every step on the ground with her bare foot.

I handed her the sword. "Everyone kept telling me that this was some sort of magical sword that could kill basically whatever, but as far as I can figure, it's just a sword."

"It's not Excalibur, is it?" Mother frowned, testing the balance of the blade.

"No." I shrugged as she quirked a brow at me. "Apparently, that's somewhere else."

She nodded once and slipped the sword into her belt, since it had no sheath. Her hand on the hilt, she lifted her chin at the dragons. "What about them? What about the sovereignty of their lands?"

I raised my brows and turned to the elder dragon. "I don't much care," I said evenly. "Would you like to contest my taking what's mine from here?"

The dragons said nothing.

"Very well, then." I slipped my arm into Neja's and turned towards the hill that would lead into the rest of Elsewhere. I paused, turning back to the dragons one more time. "Oh, and to answer your question regarding what I want. From you? Nothing. You are facing the consequences of your actions, and I think that, given Life's propensity towards irony, such a thing is punishment enough."

My mother coughed pointedly.

"Ah, yes, and please, for goodness sakes, leave my mother alone. She's the last Knight, but that won't stop her from killing every single one of you if you bother her."

With that, we walked down the hill and out of the dragon lands. I didn't think it would be long before the goblins and raiders of the barren hills bordering the idyllic landscape would realise that it was ripe for the taking. Whether the dragons emerged after that would be up to them, but as I said, consequences had to be paid.

CHAPTER 20

"Is it just me, or was that too easy?" Neja asked once we were safely beyond the remains of the border of the dragon lands. Where once fire had burned, dividing utopia and wasteland, there was now just a fine line of scorched earth. Already, I'd seen one smallish lizard the colour of rocks dart over the border. I had no doubt that there would be more than that in the days to come.

"Easy?" Mother scoffed, adjusting her grip on the sword once again. She hadn't let go of the weapon since I'd handed it to her, and every now and again I saw her knuckles whiten against the steel as she jumped at imagined sounds. "We would have been dead in another day if we stayed there any longer."

"No, not staying with the dragons," Neja said,

waving my mother's concerns off. "And they wouldn't have killed us, not with Cal's threats before he left."

"He was the one who let us be taken," my mother muttered. I pretended I didn't hear, since that was a conversation I didn't need to have with her. Neja cast a glance at me before following my cue and ignoring the accusation.

"The dragons shouldn't have let us *go* that easily," Neja said. "Keeping us as insurance against Cal's wrath? Sure. But letting us go without a fight? It was too easy."

Easy, right. I wouldn't necessarily call my trek across the dragon lands, swimming across an acid lake, fighting my own mind, as well as defeating a minotaur, escaping from the Fisher King's prison, and breaking a curse in the process, easy. I'd had many encounters with magical beings, but this ranked among them as one of the most unpleasant.

Perhaps because there were so many dead.

"I think…" Iliana said, studying her feet. "I think the dragons were afraid."

The Reapers had been following along with me and my family in silence, enough so that I hardly noticed they were there. Iliana's madness had transitioned into anxiety and uncertainty; she watched where she put every step, now, after so long in a featureless landscape with nothing to impede her way. I had a feeling the uncertainty extended past her walking. Tad, on the other hand, was almost childlike in his awe. He stared at everything, muttering under his breath about how things had changed since he came through here. He studied every rock, every scrap of life. If he didn't pace himself, he was going to burn out on sensory overload.

"Afraid!" Mother laughed. "They were afraid, so they just *gave* us up?"

"For fear of the consequences? Yes." Iliana cast a momentary glance at me before stumbling over her feet. I wished we still had our ostriches. Riding would surely be more comfortable for her.

"Consequences?" Now Mother was in fine form, her years of sarcasm and cynicism combining with her sharp wit to come out on top of any argument. It was what made people so afraid of her. "The consequences of their actions against us? What could we have possibly done to them? Well, yes, I'm a Knight, but you'll notice that there was only one of me, and the dragons were numbered in the several dozen."

"Not fear of you," Iliana snapped. She jerked her head at me. "Fear of him. Of what he'd done. Of what he will do."

A weight settled on my shoulders. I didn't really

want to be feared. But then, hadn't Death hired me in the first place because people feared him? Because he wanted to be seen in a different light?

"All I did," I said, "was to undo an injustice that the dragons started centuries ago."

"And in doing so, you made them vulnerable." Neja grabbed my hand and threaded her fingers through mine.

"Cal?" Mother asked, tone even. "Why do they fear you?"

"You know what he is," Neja scoffed, "and you still ask that? He is the heir to Death! He has Reaper powers that can kill with a touch. He—"

"I know my son," my mother said with icy clarity. "I know full well that he may be all of these things, but he is also my son. Whom I have raised. So, tell me, Calvin Montgomery Thorpe, why would they fear you?"

I stopped in my tracks and spun to face her. "They fear me because I am your son, and because, despite all those years I spent fixing other people's mistakes, painting people in a favourable light, I take after you. I see the rights and the wrongs in this world and I find it unacceptable. I can't bear to watch it unfold. I can't...I can't bear it."

In an instant, my mother had her arms wrapped around me. She hugged me tightly in an act that she hadn't done since I was a child. She wasn't the best of parents, perhaps too wrapped up in her own world, or in the world around her, to be overly concerned with mine, but she was steady. Strong. Present. I'd never once had to ask whether she loved me. Whether she would be there for me. Even when I was being scolded for something stupid that Baz had goaded me into, I knew that she was going to be there. Always.

Until the day she died.

"Perhaps I'm not the last Knight after all," she whispered in my ear. "Or perhaps there are no more Knights because the world has you, now. Your cousin may bear the mantle of Justice, but you, Cal, you are a good person."

"Do good people have blood on their hands?"

"Often more than otherwise. Because they care too much to stand aside."

She pulled back and I studied her. Couture clothes torn to pieces, her glasses smudged and scratched, hair messily braided back. Looking unlike my mother and yet entirely like her.

"Thanks, Mum," I murmured.

She nodded and stepped away entirely, pretending that the whole interaction hadn't happened. "Now. If you don't tell us where we're going, I'm going to assume you're quite lost. Are we lost, Cal?"

I looked around, studying the landscape. It

looked different, but then things always did on the way back from a journey. Still, I recognised a dip in the hills before us, one that was near a slight divot in the hill. "I know exactly where we are."

"Where are we?" Iliana asked.

"We're about a quarter mile from Casperion's den," I said, shifting the pack on my shoulder and feeling that simmering anger rising up again. "And we're going to pay him a visit."

We trekked the last distance to Casperion's den. I half-expected him to be somewhere far from here, but the rational part of my brain told me that he would remain close to the other dragons. He had wanted to be back amongst them for years beyond counting, and the one opportunity he'd had ended in total failure. He couldn't have missed the falling barriers, nor did I think he would go back to the dragons right away, given all they'd done to him. This den was a safe place for Casperion, the closest he had to a real home. He would be here.

Just to be on the safe side, though, I had Mother go first into the den. The dragon would very likely attack me on sight, but he would certainly think twice about attacking a Knight bearing a sword.

Then, maybe, we could have a nice, civilised conversation before things devolved entirely.

Mother leading the way, we went into the den of the dragon. It was just as it had been: well-lit, a gentleman's rooms complete with wooden wainscotting, dark walls, and sconces. The entry way was clear of debris, but as soon as we pushed past the heavy wooden door—unlocked, surprisingly—there was nothing but debris.

Books lay strewn across the floor, their spines bent and pages torn out. Golden trinkets were in pieces, and heavier brass statues looked as though they'd been tossed against the walls. Furniture was in pieces, crockery crunched as we walked over it. The place had been completely trashed.

"Did someone get here before we did?" Neja asked, kicking the remains of a teapot.

"It would appear that way," Tad said, crouching down and brushing his fingers over a book. "Whoever did this went for the items of sentiment rather than value. Though, a dragon's hoard is often filled with both."

Iliana fisted her hands on her hips. "How could you possibly determine that? We don't even know what valuable means, these days."

"Trust me," I said drily. "Value in Elsewhere doesn't change much over the centuries. People fight over the same trinkets as they did a thousand years ago."

I would know, given that I'd dealt with more than one of those.

My mother raised her sword and started down a

dark hallway. We hadn't been down that way before; I'd assumed it led to the dragon's private bedroom, or his hoard of jewels or something equally unintended for visitors. Now, she moved into the darkness without hesitation.

"Show yourself, dragon!" Mother called, stopping just before the light from the sitting room vanished entirely into shadow.

"Leave me alone." There was a rustling sound, and a scraping, and then a book came flying out of the tunnel, narrowly hitting my mother in the head. She pressed her mouth into a thin line.

"You would *throw* books?" she asked, indignant.

"Really? After all that he's done, the books are your primary concern?" Neja was aghast, but she wasn't shocked enough to not draw a knife. It was tiny, could barely even be considered a dagger, and somehow she'd managed to hide it from the dragons. I didn't even want to know how.

"I do work in a library, my dear," Mother said, bending down to pick up the book. She straightened its pages as best she could and set the volume down on a side table with something approaching reverence. Then, she turned back to the shadows and raised her sword. "I take it you were the one who threw all these books? Who destroyed the furniture?"

"I thought you were theorising raiders?" Casperion asked from the darkness, all dry humour and snarls.

"If there were raiders, I imagine they would be dead."

The dragon snorted. "Ah, yes, logic. A tool employed by so few people these days."

"Are you going to hide, or are you going to face me?" Mother demanded, swiping her sword through the air. It was inexpert, but did the trick. She was not going to back down, even if it meant diving into those shadows and hacking away blindly.

Casperion shifted in the darkness, moving forwards, his claws and scales rasping on the floor in a sound that was as much natural as it was a threat. Here was a creature who had managed to walk with delicate steps before, displaying the elegance of a true English gentleman, serving us tea without the tiniest threat. Now, he walked with claws extended, wings brushing against the walls, scales scraping the wood.

A threat, to remind us that he was, in fact, a dragon, and dragons should be feared.

My mother rarely responded well to threats.

Casperion emerged from the shadows by degrees: first a claw, then a flash of fang, then his broken horns as he snapped at my mother. She moved aside, but did not flinch. The two of them circled each other, backing up into the mess of the sitting room, where we could all talk.

Though, to be fair, I doubted very much that either Mother or Casperion had talking in mind.

"You have trespassed on my home," Casperion snarled. "I would know why."

"Stuff it." Neja tossed her braid over her shoulder and slid into a fighting stance. "You know exactly why we're here. Or did you think that all you've done would come without consequence?"

"Without consequence?" Casperion threw his head back and laughed. "I have been dealing with the consequences of 'all I've done' for longer than you can comprehend. I've had enough of those consequences, so I'll ask you to leave before I decide you've intruded on my hospitality."

"No," Mother said. The dragon swung around to face her.

"I beg your pardon?" he sneered. "You may be a Knight, but you are weak and untrained. You can't even hold that sword properly. Yet you *dare* to dictate to me?"

"Cal?" Iliana hissed to me, flexing her fingers, obviously ready to step in and fight. Tad, too, looked to be at the edge of violence. "Should we stop this?"

Casperion turned to me and growled, low and deep. "Yes, Deathling? Shouldn't you stop this?"

I shrugged. "I have my own grievances with you. But they can wait. I'm patient. Mother? You're welcome to go first."

Casperion didn't hesitate. He lunged for my mother, fire brimming at his maw, claws extended.

CHAPTER 21

My mother's strength was not in body, but in mind and spirit. She was wickedly intelligent and could flay any professor at any university with ease. She could play chess with masters. She could manoeuvre a conversation to her benefit without breaking a sweat. Actual, physical combat, though? Despite her success with the bandit, I realised that she was completely out of practise. She was better at dancing the two-step than fighting, and that was saying something.

At Casperion's lunge, every instinct I had was screaming at me to get in the way, to defend my defenceless mother. To *do something*. I shoved my hands into my pockets and forced myself to remain still, even as the threads of life and death made themselves apparent to me without summoning my Reaper abilities.

Mother must have been hiding secret abilities from me, because as the dragon swiped at her, she lifted the point of the sword and lunged forwards. The claws got her in the shoulder, but only barely. Her sword, though, dug in through his scales and drew blood. Casperion roared, enough to bring down the sconces on the walls.

He reared back and released a torrent of fire. Neja raised a hand and the fire extinguished. One of the fringe benefits of being a djinn, a being of smoke and fire. Though, given the sweat beading on her brow and the set to her jaw, I doubted that she could do it again. She caught my eye and managed a weak smile. I nodded my thanks.

Mother had flinched at the first stream of fire, the hesitation enough to let Casperion reach for her again with claws extended. She managed to get the sword up in time to stop an attack to her vulnerable centre, but he shredded her forearm. She let out a cry.

Casperion chuckled, drawing back and circling like a tiger. "Lady Teresa, the last Knight. No wonder your kind died out. What a pitiful offering you bring. Backed by the heir to Death himself, and you are all but defeated with two swipes of my claws."

"A Knight's power is not in the sword they bear,"

Mother panted, pressing her good hand to her wounded arm. Red seeped from between her fingers. "It is in the conviction in their hearts."

"How poetical," the dragon spat. "Poetry will not save you from dying."

He lunged, snapping his fangs. Mother managed to get the sword up between them enough that he bit down on the steel point. It embedded itself in the roof of his mouth and he shrieked, pulling his head away and wrenching the sword from Mother's grip as he did. Casperion reared on his back legs and buffeted his wings as he thrashed his head. The sword dislodged and skittered across the room to land at my feet.

Mother didn't once turn to me for help, look to me for her fallen weapon. She picked up a bit of broken crockery from the floor and leaped towards Casperion, dodging flailing claws and thrashing jaws. She managed to grab onto one of his wings and sliced the jagged ceramic through the thin membrane. Casperion's wing was clipped before he could do more than register that Mother had jumped for him.

He screamed, making the den shake in his fury. He landed on his feet with a slam and dug his claws into the floor, tearing it up in slivers. "What have you done?" he panted, turning to look at his ruined wing. They'd both been tattered before, but now the right one hung limply at his side.

"That is for lying to my son, for tricking him into leading me and Neja, completely vulnerable, into the dragon lands. That is for sending my son into an impossible situation, for *using* him as your pawn in ending your ridiculous curse." Mother threw the bloodied crockery down and ground it beneath her foot.

"For *that* you would make me flightless?" Casperion hissed, fire once again flaring at his maw.

"Our business is concluded," Mother said and turned her back on the dragon. She cradled her arm against her chest and walked back to me, chin lifted and proud. Iliana was there with a torn piece of fabric from a ruined chair to wrap my mother's wounds.

Casperion, though, was far from done with my mother. He leaped for her back, a killing fury in his gaze. He found me, instead.

His jaws connected with my shoulder and neck. He wrenched backwards, cutting my jugular wide open. In the instant between one heartbeat and the next, I died, my vision filling with a stark whiteness that was nearly blinding. I blinked, and the world righted itself. Casperion stared at me in horror as he realised what he'd done and to whom he had done it.

I didn't explode into shadows and claws and sinuous coils. I didn't tear him to pieces with fangs and fury. I didn't do anything more than reach forward and touch him on the snout, a single thread of silver grasped in my fingers. He screamed in agony, muscles spasming, as I held onto his immortality.

"When you set up the curse, you did so to protect the other dragons. None of you wanted to lose another as you had done to the Knights before. You knew you were vulnerable, for all your great power, so you retreated from the world." I knelt on the ground next to Casperion and stared him straight in the eye. He flinched. "I have no issue with running away, though it is not necessarily something that I would do. But you involved innocent people in your schemes. You bound your curse to a quest for heroes. Only a hero could break your curse, and the nature of the curse was such that no hero would knowingly do so. Therefore, their lives were forfeit from the moment they stepped into the dragon lands."

"T-they banished me," Casperion whispered, unable to look away from me.

"They did. And that was cruel. Punishing you for doing as they asked, for saving them," I acknowledged. "It did not, however, justify the use of innocents to try and break your curse."

The dragon whimpered. "What are you doing?" he asked again, barely making a sound.

"I hold your immortality in my hands," I said. "If I pull on this thread, you will become mortal. You will live a mortal span of years. You will be susceptible to injury and sickness. You will die."

"Why?" he croaked. "Why would you do this to me?"

I reached out with the hand not holding that silver thread. and stroked his muzzle. He flinched, eyes squeezing shut, but I didn't pull any further threads. Didn't take anything more than what I already held. "It would be so easy to kill you for what you've done, not only to me, but to my family. You trapped the Reapers, and you did it knowingly. Death would feel no regret at your demise for that reason alone. Neither would Life, as the Reapers are bound to both."

"Cal," Neja said, voice sharp. I turned to look at her, my grip loosening slightly. Casperion let out a quiet sigh of relief. "Is this necessary?"

Was it necessary? He needed to be taught that the lives of innocents were not fair game, that there were consequences to actions. I opened my mouth to say as such, tightening my hold once again on the threads. Casperion made a quiet keening sound.

"Please," he begged. "Don't do this."

I turned from Neja and focused my attention once more on the dragon.

"Please," he said again. "I…I'm sorry for what I did, for bringing the lives of heroes into the curse, but I could see no other way. None of us could see no other way. They couldn't see any other way to keep the curse alive but my banishment, either." He twisted his head away from me as much as he could, broken horn scraping the ground. "Please," he murmured, voice barely audible. "Please."

"It would be so easy to kill you," I said again, holding the thread so tightly that it scraped across my palm. "So easy to rip your immortality from your body and leave you vulnerable to sickness and ageing and injury…so easy to let you die."

"Cal," Neja said again, more insistent. She drew closer, hand outstretched to stop me.

"I could easily be cruel enough for that," I told the dragon. "I hold the power in my hands and it would be so easy. But the dead learn no lessons. The dead cannot feel regret or remorse or apology. And one cruelty does not often balance out another."

Here, I flicked my attention to his clipped wing. My mother was, perhaps, justified in doing what she did, but I also understood why she had stopped, why she had ground the crockery beneath her heel and walked away.

Just as Neja reached me and put her hand on my shoulder, I released the silver threads.

Casperion pulled back swiftly enough that I fell, my hands bracing me. He loomed over me, looking ready to kill me again and again and again until his anger was sated. Instead, he turned to Mother, to Neja, to the two Reapers, and back to me.

Without a word, he leaped over us all and ran for the entrance to the den, disappearing into the world beyond. I knew that I wouldn't see him again, just as I knew that he would work to undermine my existence and that of the other dragons for as long as he lived.

Neja knelt by my side and brushed back some of my hair. "Cal," she murmured, eyes sad. "Was that necessary? Killing him—"

"Would have taught him nothing," I said. "The dead learn no lessons, Neja. He needed to learn, to understand."

"And you were the one to teach him that lesson?" She frowned, studying me, and I wondered whether she believed what she asked or if she wondered whether I did.

"I am not the teacher, Life is. I am heir to Death," I said, burying my nose in her shoulder and sinking into her arms as she wrapped them around me. "I wanted to kill him. I wanted to rip his immortality from him and let him return to the other dragons weak and afraid. But…Neja, there's already been so much wrong in this affair. So many hurt. I can't bear for another to be so, and at my hand."

"I know," she murmured, rubbing my back.

It was true that the dead learned no lessons. What right was it of mine to teach those lessons, though? I was a Reaper, yes, but that put me in the area of choice, of decisions. And I was heir to Death. Death, who cared naught for a person's life, only for the instant in which they died. The instant in which they needed him. In which he severed their soul, or their lifeforce, and set it free. He didn't care whether they were murderers, or had harmed innocents. He didn't care if they were righteous or kind. Not in that instant. That moment. Yes, he interacted with people like me, like Yolanda. Yes, he was kind to those of us who needed it, but he did not get involved unless there was a slight against him.

"You really aren't human anymore, are you?" Mother asked, coming up behind me. I lifted my eyes to her and saw disappointment, sadness, and a sliver of understanding.

"No," I said. "I'm not."

Mother—no, Teresa, for perhaps my connection with her had died with my humanity—wrapped her arms around herself and nodded. "My son…tell me he's still in there somewhere?"

"He is still me. I'm still him." I stood, helping Neja

to her feet. "But I'm also something else, now. More than what I was."

"And less, too," she said. "Without that humanity…you are less, just as much as you are more."

"I'm different," I said, a compromise, her words settling into my chest like a harpoon. "And I think you are different, now, too."

She looked at the smear of blood on the ground where Casimir's wing had bled and grew pale. She turned away, pointedly not looking at the sword that lay discarded on the ground, either. Maybe that blade did hold power of a sorts, turning a person into something else. Killing a thing that couldn't be killed, only transformed.

I would be happy to let it rust in the debris of this den, forgotten forever.

"Let's get you home." I shrugged off my suit jacket and lay it over Teresa's shoulders. She held it close with her good hand. I nodded to Iliana and Tad, who had watched the proceedings in silence, uncertain. "Let's get all of you home."

Neja slipped her arm through mine and we started on the long journey home.

It took three days to make it back to the place where the wyvern had dropped us at the edges of the Northern Reaches. Without the ostriches, travelling across the wasteland was difficult at best, and severely frustrating at worst. We saw a few raiding parties of goblins and those rogues that traverse the empty places, but none of them dared approach. With five of us, two of whom wore weapons quite openly (Neja had stolen several knives and a short sword from the cache of Casperion's weapons), we were too much hassle.

The conversation on the way was mostly explaining to Tad and Iliana the changes in society since they'd been gone. Teresa and I were only really able to explain the changes in the mortal realms, since our knowledge of the history of Elsewhere was limited. Neja filled in the more magical gaps. The rise of technology seemed to fascinate Tad, while Iliana immediately decried it as a bad idea. Once I explained social media and marketing to her, I couldn't really blame her.

The wyvern trip back to the edges of Death's lands was just as terrible as I anticipated, with both Teresa and Tad getting quite sick. Neja let me hold her hand tightly; I didn't think I would ever really enjoy travel by giant flying lizard, and certainly not after having squared off with several dragons. I remembered when I first arrived in Elsewhere and Yolanda had to explain to me the difference between wyverns and dragons.

Ah, to be ignorant and naïve again. And human.

The final walk back to Death's lands was silent. Iliana and Tad were obviously nervous, shooting each other quick glances and walking close together. Teresa looked a bit ill from the after effects of the wyvern trip, but also likely because of her shredded arm. Neja had taken care of it as best she could, but we'd had limited medical supplies and were on the move. I could see her lifeforce become more orange, more strained, but she was far from dying, so I was content to wait a bit longer.

Neither one of us had spoken more than a few words to the other, unflinchingly polite and perfunctory. I tried not to think about it.

"This looks the same," Iliana said, staring at the mansion as we approached. "I mean, obviously it must have changed, but it looks the same."

"As far as I can tell, Death hasn't changed anything for centuries," I said. "It took my rock troll assistant ages to get him to even install the internet. My building, there, is the most modern thing on the estate, and it's at least a hundred years old. Though, the interior is quite up to date."

Tad reached out and took Iliana's hand. I decided to spare them further conversation and lengthened my stride, walking past them up the stairs and ringing the bell. Before my finger had even lifted from the buzzer, the door was flung open and Yolanda swept me up in a rib-crushing hug.

"You're back!" she crowed gleefully. Her boyfriend, the rock nymph Boulder, was standing behind her in the hallway, looking sheepish. "I am very glad to see you."

"Me, too," I wheezed. Yolanda put me down, still grinning. "What are you doing at the main house?"

"Oh, well..." She shuffled her feet and blushed a bright orange. "We...uh..."

"The pipes at the office burst," Boulder said. "Agravane apparently poured something down the loo that shouldn't be poured down the loo. Some sort of corrosive acid that he got sent as a gift for a marketing campaign from the dwarves. Meant for metal etching."

I could feel the blood drain from my face. "How bad is it?"

Yolanda winced. "We saved your coffee," she managed weakly.

"That's it?"

She nodded.

"And Agravane?" I asked, not quite sure whether I wanted to strangle my employee or ask after his welfare. "Where is he?"

"Shouting at the plumber," Boulder offered helpfully. "They've been at it for three days, now."

I wanted to bury my head in my hands and curse the powers that be. Given that they'd likely curse me back, I refrained. "Well, we can deal with that later," I said, my voice sounding strained even to me. "Where's Death?"

"In here, Cal." Death's cool, musical tones rang from the direction of his study. I waved my bedraggled party inside and we dutifully trouped into the study. I hadn't been in here since being hired, I realised, most of our discussions taking place in the larger, warmer library. This room was furnished with a desk, a couple of chairs, and a few pictures on the wall. There was also a sideboard graciously apportioned with alcohol of various types.

It was barely midday, but I wandered in the direction of the sideboard, anyways.

"Thaddeus," Death said, standing. "Iliana. I am so very glad to see you."

Death was tall, gaunt, with skin darker than night and empty eyes that saw beyond the void. I was struck by how much he looked like the me in my vision. The me that became Death. I took a quick sip of my whisky and relished the burn in my throat.

"We…" Tad started, but shook his head, eyes welling with tears. Iliana didn't even try to speak, just launched herself forwards and wrapped her arms around Death, burying her nose in his suit like she could memorise his scent.

"The others?" Death asked me in a quiet voice, his hand resting on Iliana's shoulder. I shook my head. Fury flashed across his face. "The one who did this?"

"The Fisher King is dead," I said. I thought of Casperion, the fear in his gaze as I'd knelt over him. "The one who bound the Fisher King is…not going to be a problem."

Death studied me, a slight frown at the corner of his mouth. Then, he nodded. "Why don't you go see to your mother and partner," he suggested. "I have much to discuss with these two."

I inclined my head, finished my whisky off in one go, and with a smile at Tad and Iliana, left them to their reunion.

"Neja," I said, catching the djinn by the wrist. "Would you take my mother to Graveltoes?" I named the Elsewhere doctor, a tiny gremlin of a creature who delighted in all things medicine, despite the magical tendencies for the denizens of Elsewhere to heal themselves.

"Sure, Cal," she said, standing on her toes to kiss my cheek. "How about tomorrow, after we've had a chance to clean up and recover, we do dinner?"

"That Peruvian place?" I asked.

"Perfect." She smiled at me, widely, full of affection and love. I bent and kissed her, squarely, soundly, just so she would know all the things I couldn't put into words. Teresa coughed pointedly, and we pulled back, smiling sheepishly. Neja retreated a bit down the hall so I could talk with my mother.

"You can't go to a human doctor," I said, gesturing to her arm, "so someone here will take care of it and then see about getting you home."

"It's fine," she said, waving a dismissive hand. "I have another week off from the library, anyways. Apparently I have accumulated quite a bit of time off."

"The dragons shouldn't bother you," I continued, "but if they do, you can call Baz or me and we'll deal with it."

"I'm perfectly capable of handling a few dragons," she sniffed.

"I'm not saying you aren't, but I'd still be happy to help. They should listen to me. Or, well, at least without too much protest."

"Cal—"

"And now that you've been to Elsewhere, you're likely to see a lot more magical creatures about the mortal realms. Unfortunately, that's just a side effect of travelling across realms. But they shouldn't bother you unless you stare too much, in which case they're likely to drag you into, well, whatever they're—"

"Calvin." Teresa grabbed my face between her hands, effectively silencing me. "I am perfectly capable of taking care of myself. Don't worry about me."

I managed a weak smile. "I'm afraid I will always worry."

"Just as I will worry about you," she said softly. "But you should know that I am proud of you. You have become so much more than I could have hoped. Never forget that."

I blinked and swallowed, words drying up in my throat.

"However," and here my mother's words turned stern. "Don't you dare forget about the monthly dinners. I cannot abide people who are late, and if you forget entirely, I will send every magical creature in the mortal realms I can find after you. Do you understand?"

"Monthly dinners?" I was aghast. "I thought you wouldn't want to...that is, after everything that happened..."

"Calvin Montgomery Thorpe!" She put her hands on her hips and glared at me. "I don't care if you are slated to become Death incarnate. I am still your mother and you *will* attend family dinners until the day I shuffle off this mortal coil. Do you understand me?"

I grinned, then swallowed it down, since I knew that was not the reaction she wanted. "Yes, Mother." I hugged her, gently, firmly, then pulled away. "I love you."

"I love you, too." She turned to Neja. "I am ready to see your doctor, now. My arm hurts."

Neja beamed at me and led my mother away. Teresa didn't spare one backwards glance, her shoulders back and head held high. I chuckled as they marched out the door.

Family.

I shook my head. What would we do without them?

—

About a month after returning from the dragon lands, I met Death in the library. The plumbing disaster in my offices and flat was still being repaired, and the interior would need to be completely redone. Yolanda was staying with Boulder, working from home. Agravane was out on assignment, photographing some dryads for their new campaign. It turned out that Agravane was quite the photographer, and his clients liked the work he did a lot, so I forgave him for the plumbing.

It did mean that I had to share the house with Death and his two dogs, Mischief and Mayhem. I didn't really mind.

"Ah, there you are, Cal," Death said, peering at me over a snifter of brandy. He sat before a roaring fire, looking every bit the country gentleman in his wool suit and fine silk cravat. I hoped that one day he'd give me the name of his tailor, but as yet it hadn't happened. I lay hints down as often as I could, just in case, though.

"Here I am," I replied, sinking into a chair. Tempest, my ghost, lay curled up before the fire. Her ear twitched as I sat, but she remained blissfully asleep. Mischief ran up and put her nose on my lap, wagging her tail hopefully. I scratched her ears and sighed. "Very well. If you go get the ball, I will throw it for you."

"Ball!" she cried and ran off, her brother Mayhem not far behind her.

"You'll be at it all day," Death promised. "Those two have more energy than even I know what to do with."

Still, when Mischief brought her ball, I threw it.

"I wondered if we could talk about, ah, what happened," Death said after I'd thrown the ball twice more. The dogs were now quietly wrestling with each other to see who got to deliver the ball to me next. "With the dragons."

"Ah," I said. "What, exactly, would you like to discuss?"

"You did the right thing," he answered. "I know—I knew, that is—what I was sending you into when I told you to free the Reapers from the Fisher King. I knew that you would be breaking that curse, that you would be bringing down the barrier. I knew that the world would change because of my need for… well, I couldn't leave the others there."

"You never considered that I would fail?" The thought had occurred to me, when I'd returned home and had time to think. I had wondered what Death had actually expected me to do, how much he knew. A small weight lifted from my shoulders when I realised that the blame for the changing of the world—and it *was* changing, dramatically—was not entirely my fault. Was not entirely my doing.

"You have never once failed me, Cal," Death said, taking a sip of brandy. It was a phrase said with such casualness that it stole my breath. I frowned. Death turned to me, fixing me in his empty stare. "Truly."

"Then…?" What was there to discuss.

"Do you regret it?"

I froze. The words were so similar to the ones I'd heard in my dream on the island, brought about by the ghost. I waited for Death to say more, to clarify, to ask whether it was that I regretted freeing the dragons from their self-imposed prison, or something else. He said nothing.

"No," I said at last. I regretted neither the dragons nor coming here. "No, I have no regrets."

Death smiled. "I'm glad. There will be many such decisions in your future. But thoughts of the future are for another day. Today, I'd much rather sit here and talk about religion."

I spluttered, glad I didn't have a drink. Mayhem took that moment to drop the slobbery ball in my lap. I winced, but threw it anyways. "Religion?"

"What a person believes about the afterlife can often influence their thoughts on death and dying. I thought it might be an interesting discussion, given that you're going to take over for me. If you'd rather, I could assign reading." He tilted his head, a wry smile touching his mouth.

"No," I said, relaxing a bit. "I think I'd like to just sit and talk for a while."

"Good," Death said. "Let me get you a drink."

I'd like to say that things settled down after that. I'd like to say that Tad and Iliana fit in perfectly with things as they were, that I went to dinner with my mother and Baz every month, that Yolanda and Boulder got married, that I formally promoted Agravane from junior marketer to head marketer. I'd like to say that time danced onwards with the inexorable force of contentment.

Some of it would even be true.

But, as always, things are never quite as they seem. And there were too many things to do for a quiet life. Such was my lot. I complained, loudly, to anyone who would listen, but the truth is, I wouldn't change it for anything.

I chose this life once, and I would choose it again. Or, well, I would choose this death.

In a heartbeat.

A NOTE

I can't believe that this is the end of the series. On Behalf of Death has been such a huge part of my writing journey and I am so thrilled to be able to share this with everyone. I loved writing these books. I know they're a bit ridiculous, and I know that they're not very serious (except when they are, in which case they are Very Serious), but they were the books that I needed to write.

With that being said, I am going to be transitioning into a more epic style of fantasy, with a focus on disability representation. There are so many people in the world whose stories deserve to be told, and I hope that you'll join me on my journey in telling those stories. Cal will still be there, inevitable, when the time comes.

Thank you for everyone who has helped support this series and read this collection of shenanigans. I could not have done any of this without you.

Best,

Evelyn Grimald "E.G." Stone

ABOUT THE AUTHOR

Evelyn Grimald "E.G." Stone is an independent author, editor, and linguist who has been writing, creating and causing vast amounts of trouble since a young age. When not writing, she is off musing about the workings of languages—both real and created—or reading and sewing. E.G. reads voraciously, much to the confusion of her two dogs and two cats. Weird, nerdy, perhaps a little crazy, she is having a grand old time writing, reading, editing, musing on language, and, naturally, continuing her endeavours in causing trouble.

facebook.com/egswriter

instagram.com/egswriter

amazon.com/stores/Evelyn-Grimald-
Stone/author/B07HZ3M82C